"I hate to ask this, but..."

Brooke looked uncomfortable.

"What?" Jonas asked.

"Your son had a dead woman's cell phone in his room. Do you think he had anything to do with her death?"

Jonas stepped back, her words hurting more than if she'd slapped him. "What? No. Of course not." He raked a hand through his hair, hating the flash of doubt that raced through him. "No. I mean my son has been getting in some trouble lately, but he'd never hurt—kill—someone over a stupid phone."

She held up a hand. "Just had to ask."

The anger fizzled as fast as it had flamed. "I understand why you might ask that, but no. It's not possible."

"Then how did the phone wind up under his mattress two months after its owner was found murdered?"

* * *

CAPITOL K-9 UNIT:
These lawmen solve the toughest cases with the help of their brave canine partners

Protection Detail—Shirlee McCoy, March 2015
Duty Bound Guardian—Terri Reed, April 2015
Trail of Evidence—Lynette Eason, May 2015
Security Breach—Margaret Daley, June 2015
Detecting Danger—Valerie Hansen, July 2015
Proof of Innocence—Lenora Worth, August 2015

Lynette Eason is a bestselling, award-winning author who makes her home in South Carolina with her husband and two teenage children. She enjoys traveling, spending time with her family and teaching at various writing conferences around the country. She is a member of RWA (Romance Writers of America) and ACFW (American Christian Fiction Writers). Lynette can often be found online interacting with her readers. You can find her at facebook.com/lynette.eason and on Twitter at @lynetteeason.

Books by Lynette Eason

Love Inspired Suspense

Capitol K-9 Unit

Trail of Evidence

Wrangler's Corner

The Lawman Returns

Family Reunions

Hide and Seek
Christmas Cover-Up
Her Stolen Past

Rose Mountain Refuge

Agent Undercover
Holiday Hideout
Danger on the Mountain

Visit the Author Profile page at Harlequin.com for more titles

TRAIL OF EVIDENCE

LYNETTE EASON

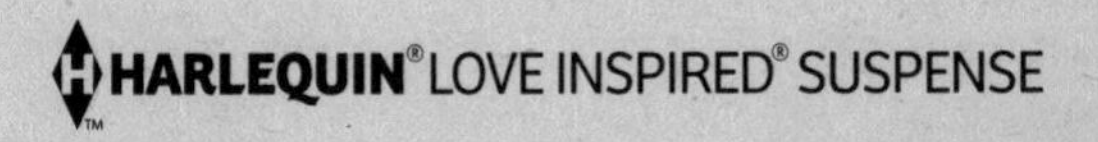

Special thanks and acknowledgment are given to Lynette Eason for her contribution to the Capitol K-9 Unit miniseries

TM LOVE INSPIRED BOOKS

ISBN-13: 978-0-373-44666-7

Trail of Evidence

This edition published by arrangement with Love Inspired Books.

www.Harlequin.com

Printed in U.S.A.

This means that it is not the children of the flesh
who are the children of God, but the children of the promise
are counted as offspring.

—*Romans* 9:8

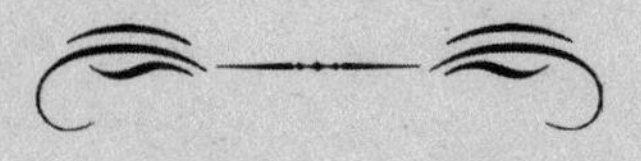

Dedicated to my Lord and Savior, Jesus Christ. Thank You for giving me the passion to write and to write for You.

ONE

Veterinarian Jonas Parker jerked from his slight doze and lay still in the recliner where he'd crashed only a few minutes earlier shortly after midnight. He'd spent the night treating a longtime client's Doberman, who'd gotten hit by a car. A few lacerations and a couple of broken bones later, the dog now rested in the kennel at the office and Jonas had come home to get some much-needed rest. Only now he was hearing things. His ears honed in on the noises of his house and he frowned, wondering what had awakened him.

Silence echoed back at him.

Annoyance rushed through him. He'd just gotten relaxed enough to maybe fall asleep, and his house settling had disturbed him. He snorted. Earplugs might be a good investment. He closed his eyes and let out a low breath.

Crash.

Jonas shot into a sitting position as his blood pounded through his veins.

That wasn't the house settling. Someone was *in* his house. Upstairs.

Felix! He had to get to Felix, his thirteen-year-old son. He froze, his thoughts scrambling. No. Wait. It was Saturday night. Felix was sleeping over at a friend's. A flash of relief, then determination made his heart kick up speed.

Who was it? What did the intruder want? Money? Jewelry? Moving as silently as possible, Jonas rose from the recliner and stood, fingers clenching and unclenching at his sides.

A weapon.

He needed to be able to defend himself.

Where was his phone? He had to call for help. And get out.

The stairs creaked. He stopped at the edge of the room.

To get to either the front door or the back, he would have to go through the kitchen. Which meant passing the stairs.

While his adrenaline pounded, Jonas thought hard. His cell phone was on the kitchen counter. He didn't have a landline.

Soft footfalls on the steps reached his ears as though someone didn't want to make a lot of noise, but wasn't very skilled at being quiet.

Jonas grabbed the nearest thing he could use as a weapon from the built-in shelf. Felix's track meet trophy, his son's pride and joy. Hefting it in his left hand, he decided to bolt for the kitchen, grab his phone from the counter and keep going out the back door. He'd avoid a confrontation if at all possible but he needed to get help on the way.

Grab the phone, get out and call for help. A good plan. He slipped past the bottom of the steps, praying the darkness hid him from whoever was on them. In the kitchen, moonlight filtering from the window over the sink illuminated the way.

The floor creaked behind him.

A hard hand centered itself in the middle of his back and a hard shove propelled him into the kitchen table. Jonas bounced, stumbled and crashed into the refrigerator. Felix's trophy tumbled from his fingers. Fury boiled through him and he spun, striking out, praying to hit something. He landed a hard fist on his attacker's face.

A hiss of surprise and a curse reached his ears.

Jonas managed to grab the trophy once more. Then the feel of something hard and cold against his left cheek froze him. "I have a son," he whispered. "He needs me."

"Give me the phone."

"What phone?" Jonas clutched the trophy, his mind racing.

"Give me the phone!"

The weapon moved, slipping from his cheek. Jonas brought the base of the heavy trophy up and moved sideways at the same time. He connected with the attacker's stomach, heard a whoosh, then the gun clattering on the floor. The man cursed, swept his hand out and grabbed the gun. Jonas swung the trophy once more, connected. The intruder gave a harsh cry and bolted for the door.

Jonas panted and rose to go after him. Then thought of his son and stopped.

He grabbed his cell phone from the counter and dialed 911.

Brooke Clark pushed the laptop away and rubbed her gritty eyes. One in the morning and she was on her laptop? She needed to be sensible and get some sleep. But her adrenaline was still high even though her eyes longed to shut.

She'd just walked in the door an hour ago from a crime scene where Mercy, her very skilled K-9 golden retriever, had done her job well. She'd recovered some key evidence in a bank robbery and once testing was done on the glove, Brooke knew the DNA would put the criminal away.

Unfortunately, sleep would have to wait. She groaned, settled into the recliner and decided to keep working on the case that had caused her and her team no end of frustration.

Congressman Harland Jeffries continued to pound home the fact that his son's murder still wasn't solved. Late one night two months ago, someone had killed Michael Jeffries. Michael wasn't just the congressman's son, but was also a well-respected lawyer. The congressman had come upon the scene, his son on the ground, shot, and the murderer standing over Michael's body. The killer had turned the gun on the congressman and shot him, leaving him for dead. Only Harland hadn't died. He'd lived to tell the story and demand justice for his son. Unfortunately, darkness had prevented the congressman from seeing the murderer's face, so the hunt was still on to find the person responsible.

She and the other members of the Capitol K-9 team wouldn't be granted rest until the case was solved. Brooke loved her job, but frustration built at the lack of progress when it came to finding answers. She flipped the page in the file. Rosa Gomez, Congressman Jeffries's housekeeper, was also connected to the case. Shortly before the shooting, Rosa had been found dead at the base of the cliffs in President's Park. "Which hasn't been technically proved to be murder. It could have been an accident," she told Mercy. The dog yawned, then gave a low whine and nudged against her hand. The animal's affection made her smile and run her hand over Mercy's silky soft ears.

Mercy, her sweet—and super smart—golden retriever.

Highly trained, Mercy and Brooke were partners in the elite Capitol K-9 Unit based in Washington, DC. Mercy specialized in retrieving evidence. Brooke sighed. She wished there were some evidence to be retrieved in either Michael Jeffries's murder or Rosa Gomez's death. "It's all right, girl. Just because I'm up doesn't mean you have to lose out on a good night's sleep." Mercy heaved a sigh and settled at Brooke's feet. Then rose to pad to the door and back.

"You're restless, too, huh?" Brooke got up from the recliner and went to open the door for Mercy. The dog bounded into the fenced yard, and Brooke stared out into the dark night. She shivered at the chill. March was a cold month in DC, and Brooke hadn't grabbed her coat. She watched Mercy sniff and weave in and out of the bushes lining the fence. The trees beyond offered a sense of privacy and security, one of the reasons Brooke had purchased the home.

She pulled the door shut behind her and sat on the cement steps, wrapping her arms around her middle. Maybe the cold would revive some of her dead brain cells. Her thoughts were like a dog with a bone. She couldn't keep her mind from gnawing on the Jeffries case.

Harland Jeffries was about to push Gavin, her captain, over the edge. Gavin was a good man, a professional in every sense of the word. Brooke respected how he had managed to hold on to his temper when it came to the congressman's incessant demands on Gavin's time. She stood. "Mercy, come."

The dog bounded over to her and sat at her feet, ears perked. Brooke gave those ears a good rub and let the dog back into the house. Poor Gavin. He was really torn. She knew he was between a rock and a hard place. He had a lot of respect for the congressman. Harland had been a mentor to Gavin, and Gavin loved the man like a father. It was tearing him up not to be able to give him some answers.

She forced herself to head to bed. She'd count sheep if she had to. Or review the case notes while snuggling under the warm down comforter. Maybe then she'd doze off.

And maybe pigs would start flying.

Jonas shut the door as the police officers headed toward their squad car. He appreciated the fast response to his 911 call, but the officers had basically checked out the scene, taken a few pictures of the dumped drawer in Felix's room, then told him to be thankful he wasn't hurt and nothing was missing. Oh, and to call if anything else happened.

Right.

He sighed and reached back to massage the area at the base of his skull. He needed a vacation. A stress-reducing getaway. But Felix was in school for another three weeks before his spring break.

Maybe then.

He trudged up the stairs to Felix's room and took another look around. The drawer on the floor, the unmade bed, an unfinished 3-D puzzle of the capitol building. He sighed and picked up Felix's favorite sweatshirt and tossed it across the footboard of the bed. A pair of jeans and a hoodie joined the sweatshirt.

His eyes caught on the picture on his son's nightstand. Felix had been about two years old. He was laughing up at Shannon, his mother and Jonas's ex-wife. It had been a happy time in his young life, Jonas's life, too. Neither

Felix nor Jonas had known the trouble that would come just a few short years away. Trouble brought on by Shannon and her commitment-phobic ways.

Jonas sighed, flipped off the light and headed to his own room. He crawled between the sheets, forcing his muscles to relax, his mind to drift into prayer. Until he remembered the crash he heard. The drawer to Felix's nightstand had been yanked out and dumped. His heart thudded. The officers had come to the same conclusion he had. The intruder had already been in his house when he'd arrived home. Either the man hadn't heard him come in and drop into the recliner—or he hadn't cared and just continued his search.

Jonas debated whether to get up and clean up the drawer or wait until later.

It would wait. He drifted. Sleep beckoned.

At least until the strange beeping jerked him awake again.

Jonas sat straight up, his adrenaline spiking once more. Heart thundering in his chest, he grabbed the baseball bat he'd placed on the floor near his bed and swung his legs over the side. He stood and padded on bare feet to the door.

The faint beeping sounded again. Then all was silent.

Jonas's fingers flexed around the bat. He grabbed his cell phone with his left hand and shoved it into the waistband of his knit shorts.

More beeping.

Jonas followed the sound into his son's bedroom two doors down from his. He stood in the doorway and listened.

Nothing.

And then he heard it again. Louder this time. He was definitely closer.

Jonas flipped the light on and blinked against the sudden brightness. When his eyes adjusted, he dropped to his knees on the hardwood floors and scanned the area under Felix's dresser. Finding nothing, he rose and moved to his son's bedside table. The drawer still lay on its side. He grabbed the small flashlight and went to his knees once again.

Jonas flashed the light under the bed. The beeping sounded right next to his ear. He lifted the mattress, separating it from the box springs, and froze, puzzled. A cell phone? He snagged it and dropped the mattress back into place. Fingers curled around the phone, he lifted it up to study it. "Who does this belong to?" he muttered. One of Felix's friends? But why would Felix have it hidden under his mattress? Had he stolen it?

Jonas snapped the light off and carried the phone into his bedroom. He flipped on the lamp and sank onto the bed, his eyes still on the device. Low battery. Hence the beeping.

He touched the screen to bring the phone to life. A picture stared back at him. A woman holding a baby. He frowned as recognition hit him. He knew that woman. He'd seen her on the news, hadn't he? And in the papers. He got up and strode into the kitchen to grab the newspaper from the counter.

There. Right on the front page. Housekeeper for Congressman Harland Jeffries, Rosa Gomez had been found at the bottom of the cliffs in President's Park approximately two months ago and the investigation continued to make front-page news as new evidence came to light. The Capitol K-9 Unit had been working the case and the story had stayed hot, the media constantly reminding everyone that this case hadn't been solved yet.

And someone had just broken into his house looking for a phone. He stared at the device. Could he have been looking for this one?

His thoughts went immediately to Brooke Clark, a Capitol K-9 Unit team member who was working the case.

An officer and a beautiful woman. He pushed aside the personal thoughts and focused on what to do about this phone. Right now, he couldn't worry about how Felix had gotten ahold of it, he had to turn it in.

And he knew just the person he wanted to give it to.

Brooke jerked out of the light sleep she'd managed to fall into sometime between her last sip of warm tea and a prayer for divine help in solving her case. She rolled to grab her phone from the end table. "'Lo?"

"I woke you up. I'm sorry."

Sleep fled. She sat up. "Jonas Parker?" Her heart stuttered. Just saying his name brought back a flood of memories. Both wonderful and…painful. Along with boatloads of regret. The same feelings that rushed through her every time she saw or spoke to him. Which hadn't been too long ago. Maybe a month? Amazing that she had no trouble pulling the memory of his voice from the depths of her tired mind. But then why would she? She often dreamed of him, their past times together. And they hadn't even dated. Not once. She blinked. "What's wrong?"

"You're working the case about the congressman's son's death, aren't you?"

"Yes. Michael Jeffries." She cleared her throat. "You called me at four o'clock in the morning to ask that?"

"No, I called to tell you that I think I found something that you might need for your investigation."

"What?"

"A phone with a picture of Rosa Gomez and her two-year-old son as the wallpaper."

Fully awake now, Brooke swung her legs over the edge of the bed. At the foot of the bed, Mercy lifted her head and perked her ears. "Where did you find the phone?" she asked.

The fact that Rosa's wallet and phone hadn't been found with her body had raised a lot of questions. Like had her fall from the cliffs been an accident or murder? And if it had been an accident, where were the items? And if it had been murder, had the murderer stolen them?

Another question: Was Rosa's death connected to the shooting of her boss, Congressman Jeffries, and the murder of his son? So far, they had few suspects, one being a senator's daughter, Erin Eagleton. She'd disappeared the night of the murder and her starfish charm, engraved with her initials, had been found at the scene. Brooke was glad that Rosa's child was now in the custody of his aunt, but so many questions remained. Maybe the phone Jonas had would answer some of them.

"Ah… Well, that's the problem. And one of the reasons I called you."

"Come on, Jonas, tell me."

"I found the phone under my son's mattress."

TWO

Brooke threw the covers back, wide awake now. "You found it where?" Surely he hadn't said—

"Under his mattress."

He *had* said it.

"And that's not all," he continued. "Someone broke into my house tonight and demanded I give him 'the phone.' Of course I didn't know what he was talking about at the time, but now I'm feeling quite sure he meant the one I'm holding."

Brooke struggled to process everything. "Are you all right? Is Felix okay?" Pain shafted through her. She pushed it away. When she'd met him, Jonas was working as a vet at the K-9 dog training facility. He'd been divorced, with a young son. And he hadn't made any secret of the fact that he found her attractive. She'd felt the same spark but had smothered it as best she could. Jonas had also never made any secret of the fact that he wanted a houseful of children.

Children she could never give him thanks to a hysterectomy at the age of eighteen. The car wreck that had killed her parents had also killed her dream of being a mother. She swallowed hard and pushed the thoughts away. She'd dealt with this, and she didn't need to dwell on it or rehash it. What was done was done. She'd moved on. And so had Jonas. And yet—

Over the course of the past eight years, they'd run into each other, but had never exchanged more than a few pleasantries. She'd climbed the ladder in law enforcement and had landed her dream job with the Capitol K-9 Unit when it had been formed a few short years ago. For some reason tonight's call stirred up old longings and questions about what might have been. And the guilt that she'd never explained why she'd run from him.

"Felix wasn't here," he said. "He's spending the night with a friend."

"But you weren't hurt?" She blinked away the past.

"No, I managed to chase him off."

Relief hit her. "Good for you." She bit her lip. "All right. I'll come over and get the phone."

"Now?"

"I don't want to take a chance on whoever you scared off coming back. We need to get that phone into the right hands so it doesn't fall into the wrong ones."

He paused. "I hadn't thought about that. Bring your dog. Maybe she can pick up the intruder's scent."

Of course he knew about Mercy. Just like he knew she worked for the Capitol K-9 Unit. So. He'd been keeping up with her, too. Interesting. "She'll be with me." She glanced at the clock. "It should take me about ten to fifteen minutes to get there."

"I'll be waiting."

Brooke hung up, her mind spinning. Jonas Parker had called her. Jonas needed help and he'd called *her*. Just the thought of seeing him again on more than a passing basis made her palms sweat and her pulse beat a little faster.

Mercy whined and hopped to the floor where she sat, head cocked, ears lifted. Her tail thumped the floor as though to say, "I'm ready when you are."

Brooke dressed in record time, popped a K-cup in her Keurig and pulled her travel mug down from the cabinet. Time for the strong stuff. While the coffee brewed, she gathered her bag and Mercy's leash.

Ten minutes later, she was in her truck and headed for Jonas's house. A fact that continued to make her blood hum and stir the memories of a time she'd tried to forget. She'd been a rookie with the DC police department's K-9 unit and he'd been interning as a vet at the dog training facility. They'd crossed paths often enough to strike up a friendship. When Jonas had expressed an interest in being more than friends, she'd spooked and run, canceling out on a date at the last minute and then finding excuses not to see him alone again. She hadn't handled it well, too caught up in her own insecurities and hurt to really consider how her actions would affect him. He'd been embarrassed and hurt and they'd parted ways.

And yet he'd called her about finding evidence in the case she and the Capitol K-9 team were working so hard on.

The pressure was on to find Michael Jeffries's killer and Congressman Jeffries's shooter—most likely the same person. Tension was thick, but Brooke had no doubts about her team. They were the best. They'd find the killer. She just hoped it would be before he struck again.

Jonas paced the den, his heart pounding, his palms slick. What was he thinking?

That he wanted to see Brooke Clark. Vaguely he wondered if he should feel guilty for being secretly glad he'd had a legitimate excuse to call her. Then he pushed the guilt away. His divorce had been final ten years ago. He'd mourned the loss of his marriage, but finally, with the help of a recovery group at his church, realized he'd done everything he could to keep his marriage together. The fact was, it had ended and it was time for him to move on.

Why his heart had settled on Brooke Clark was something that had him stumped. But she'd been the reason he'd sought out the recovery group in the first place. He'd needed someone to tell him it was all right for him to find companionship. Date again.

And then Brooked ditched him. She'd simply canceled their last date and had avoided him until he gave up trying to get in touch with her. And he'd never figured out why. Maybe it was time to get some answers. Even if they were ones he didn't want to hear.

A car door slammed.

He tensed and went to the window to push aside the curtain so he could see out. As always, his heart did that funny little beat when he saw her. A petite woman in her early thirties with short black hair. She still looked the same. Slightly older, but not much. And definitely still beautiful.

Brooke. She was here. Her golden retriever, Mercy, leaped to the ground and shook herself, her brown eyes on Brooke, waiting for instructions. Jonas had followed her career and watched her climb the ranks in law enforcement. He was proud of her.

He opened the front door. Brooke looked up and caught his gaze and Jonas blinked. He hadn't forgotten how blue her eyes were. On the contrary, he remembered every detail about her. But those eyes always rendered him speechless when first making contact. For a moment they just stood and stared. Then she smiled and walked toward him. “Hi, Jonas. Good to see you again.”

Jonas took a step and, in a bold move, wrapped her in a hug. Her scent surrounded him, old feelings rushed back. And she didn’t push him away. He took a deep breath. “It’s really good to see you, too, Brooke. Come on in.”

Brooke swept past him and he heard her give the dog a low command. Mercy sat. Jonas stepped inside and shut the door behind him.

She looked around. “So what happened?”

Jonas pinched the bridge of his nose. “It’s a bit of a story. Would you like to go into the den and have a seat?”

“I’d rather not. Did the intruder leave anything behind? Touch anything that his scent would be on?”

So. It was going to be all business then. All right. He could take a hint. Jonas tightened his jaw then relaxed it. She was here to help, not socialize. The fact that she hadn’t pulled away from his embrace encouraged him. First things first. “I was in the recliner in the den when I heard a crash. It came from my son’s room. The intruder had pulled out one of the drawers from Felix’s nightstand. It was on the floor when I went in.”

“Then let’s start there.”

“Of course.” Jonas led her into Felix’s bedroom, once again giving thanks that his son hadn’t been home at the time of the break-in.

She focused in on the drawer on the floor. “I guess I don’t have to ask which drawer.”

“No. Guess not. I just left it alone. Once I decided to call you, I didn’t want to cover up any smells.” He paused. “I also hit the guy with Felix’s trophy so his scent may be on there, too.”

She shot him an admiring glace. “Good job. Okay, we’ll see what we can do.”

Jonas stepped back and let them go to work. He watched, marveling at the team, how well they worked together. “You’re very good at what you do, aren’t you?”

She turned. “We’re one of the best.” She said it in all sincerity, without a hint of boasting or pride. Just stated a fact. He liked that about her.

“You didn’t ask for my address.”

She blinked, then cleared her throat. “Excuse me?”

“You didn’t have to ask for my address. You already knew it.”

“I looked it up in the police database.”

“Of course.” Now he felt embarrassed. “For a moment there, it gave me hope.”

“Hope?”

“Hope that you’d thought about me. Hope that…I don’t know, that maybe we could be friends again.”

“We never stopped being friends.”

He shook his head. “Of course we did. Friends do stuff together, hang out, enjoy each other’s company. We went from friends to acquaintances that shared a nod of acknowledgement whenever we ran into each other. That’s not friendship.”

Brooke bit her lip and turned away. “This isn’t what I came over here for. Let me just do my job.”

Disappointment flooded him. He’d pushed too hard, too fast. He was coming across desperate and it wasn’t that; he just had questions. Questions that would have to wait. “No problem.”

Once she finished going through the house, she let Mercy out the door the intruder had exited. Mercy trotted down the street, nose alternating between the ground and the air. She stopped several houses down and sat.

Brooke called to her and Mercy hurried to her side. "She's lost the scent. Most likely the guy had a car waiting right where Mercy sat down. He climbed in and off they went."

He nodded. He'd expected as much. He handed her the phone. "The battery is at two percent. It won't last much longer. There may be a charger in his room. I didn't think to look."

She studied it. "It's fine. Chargers are easy to come by." She looked up. "Did you find a wallet belonging to Rosa?"

"No. Just the phone."

"I hate to ask this, but..." She looked uncomfortable.

"What?"

"Well, Rosa's wallet was missing, too. Do you think Felix could have hurt Rosa to get her phone and wallet?"

Jonas stepped back, her words hurting more than if she'd slapped him. "What? No. Of course not." He raked a hand through his hair, hating the flash of doubt that raced through him. He lifted his chin. "No. He's a thirteen-year-old boy, he's not perfect. And I mean he's been getting in some trouble lately, but that's just because he's never gotten over his mother's leaving, never truly accepted the fact that she would do that. He'd never hurt—kill—someone over a stupid phone." Anger flared.

She held up a hand. "Just had to ask. And I didn't necessarily mean that he killed her on purpose. It could have been an accident and he was too scared to tell anyone what happened."

"No, no way. Absolutely not." She nodded, her eyes on his. The anger fizzled as fast as it had flamed. "I understand why you might ask that, but no. It's not possible. If something like that had happened, Felix would have come to me." Wouldn't he?

"Then how did the phone wind up under his mattress two months after its owner was found murdered?"

The question hit him hard. He swallowed. "I don't know, but I know we have to find out."

"We need to talk to Felix."

She held the phone up. "We need to turn this in, too." She headed to the bedroom door when Jonas heard a loud roar and felt the house rock beneath his feet.

Mercy barked. Brooke fell to her knees. She thought she heard Jonas calling to her just before something struck her shoulder, her leg, her cheek. Pain lanced through her. "Get out! We have to get out."

Jonas's hand wrapped her upper arm. She realized he'd fallen, too; he'd just recovered faster than she. Smoke seared her lungs, but nothing felt hot.

"Are you all right?" Jonas coughed as he pulled her toward the door.

"Fine. Mercy, heel!" The dog slunk on her belly to Brooke's side. She pulled her shirt up over her nose and mouth. Jonas did the same. She grabbed one of Felix's shirts from his bed and wrapped it around the animal's mouth and nose, leaving it loose enough for her to breathe while filtering the smoke.

"Smoke is rolling in fast," he said.

"Do you see any flames?"

"No. Let me lead you, I know the layout." He coughed and together they made their way down the stairs, ready to turn and flee back up at the first sign of fire. Finally, they hit the bottom of the steps. Jonas led her toward the door. Mercy hugged her side and she kept one hand on the head of her faithful friend.

Jonas opened the door and she yanked him back in to slam it. Her shoulder throbbed with the movement.

"What are you doing?" he asked.

"Do you have a back door?"

"Yes."

"Let's use that."

She could barely see his puzzled expression, but gave silent thanks that he didn't argue with her, just kept his firm grip on her good arm and led her toward the back of the house and into a sunroom. Her leg throbbed, but nothing was broken and she moved through the house with minimal pain.

Smoke still filled the air, but she could breathe much better here. He opened the door and they stepped out into the night. Fresh air hit her and she sucked in a deep breath even as her mind spun. She pulled her arm free, then slid her hand down to wrap her fingers around his. "Come on," she croaked.

They raced away from the house, her leg protesting the movement, but nothing bad enough to stop her from getting to safety. Sirens already sounded and Brooke suspected one of the neighbors had heard the blast and called 911. Jonas had a nice fenced-in yard that backed up to his neighbor's. They moved to the edge of the property.

Brooke turned to see smoke billowing from the den window, but no flames. "I'm going to see if I can spot anyone trying to get away from the house." She took off with Mercy at her heels. Jonas's protest registered, but she needed to see. Rounding the corner of the house, she stopped and looked up and down the street. Neighbors stood on their porches and some in the street as they watched the commotion. The first fire truck screamed to a stop at the curb. Brooke's gaze bounced from person to person. Curiosity and concern graced the faces of the onlookers. No one seemed particularly satisfied.

Jonas stepped up beside her. "See anything?"

"No. Do you see anyone who shouldn't be here? Anyone you don't recognize?"

"I'm…um…probably not the best person to ask."

"Why?"

"Because I'm a lousy neighbor." He gave an embarrassed shrug. "I work and I spend time with Felix—when he lets me anyway. I hate yard maintenance so I hire someone to do it."

"Which means you're not working in the yard and talking with people out for an evening or weekend walk."

"Exactly."

She nodded and approached the fire captain. "We were in that house. We're fine. There's no one else inside."

The man turned, his concerned gaze landing on the two of them. "Are you sure?"

"Positive."

One of the firemen stepped out the front door and motioned to one of his buddies. "Captain?"

"Yeah."

Jonas and Brooke moved closer. Mercy stayed by her side. Brooke wanted to hear what was said.

"It was a Molotov cocktail. When it was tossed through the window, it landed in the fireplace." The man shook his head. "Never seen anything like it. There's a lot of smoke, but not any fire damage to speak of. Looks like it wasn't meant to burn, just cause a lot of smoke."

Jonas breathed out. Brooke laid a hand on his forearm. He looked at her. “You’re right,” he said. “They came back.”

Brooke pulled the cell phone Jonas had found from her pocket. “I think it’s time to ask Felix where he got this phone and who knows he has it.” She switched to her business phone. “And we’re going to get someone to watch your house tonight. I don’t think we were smoked out by accident. Whoever threw that in there knew what they were doing. It’s possible they plan to come back and search the place.”

“So then I’m not sleeping here.”

“Not with the smoke and the danger. You’re going someplace safe.”

THREE

Brooke sat in the SUV next to Nicholas Cole, a fellow Capitol K-9 member, and kept her eyes on Jonas's house. It looked empty and deserted. Just the way they wanted it to look. If someone planned to return to the scene of the crime, she and Nicholas would be waiting. "What time is it?"

"Five minutes later than the last time you asked," he said.

"You sound like my grandfather."

"You sound like a five-year-old. It's 4:45 a.m. An hour of the night that should have me in bed dreaming of a vacation on the beach, not conducting a stakeout."

She snorted and swung her gaze back to the area around the house, looking for movement, a flash of light. Anything. And got nothing.

She could hear the dogs breathing behind her. They were suited up, their protective vests on and ready to go. And so was Brooke. She itched for a break, a chance to go after someone who could give them a break in this case.

Instead of going after Felix to question him about the phone, they'd simply sent an officer to watch the house where he was staying. Felix was safe for now and if the person who wanted the phone came back and they caught him, Felix would never have to know how fortunate it was he chose to spend the night away from home. Talking to the boy could wait until morning. Catching the person who wanted the phone was priority. The sun would be up in a couple of hours, but Brooke just had a feeling something was going to happen.

Her heart, protected by the Kevlar vest she'd donned earlier, thumped a heavy rhythm. Anticipation swept through her. It was about time something good happened.

General Margaret Meyer apparently thought so, too. The Capitol K-9 Unit existed because of her. Her current position as the White House Special In-House Security Chief gave her a lot of power and leeway. Gavin reported straight to her and she expected top-notch results from her team. Which they gave her. When Gavin had presented her with the need for some manpower due to a possible break in the case, she'd been more than happy to spare Nicholas from his current duties at the White House to help Brooke track down the lead.

"So who is this guy?" Nicholas asked. He sipped on a drink they'd picked up from the local gas station.

"What guy?" Brooke knew exactly who he meant, but she needed to buy some time to figure out just how much she wanted to reveal about Jonas. Then again, it wasn't like there was that much to say. Nicholas simply lifted a brow and she shrugged. "We met about eight years ago. He was doing an internship and I was a rookie K-9 cop."

"And you hit it off?"

"We did."

"Was it serious?"

She hesitated. It had been serious. Too serious. "We were friends. We had a lot in common and spent some time together, but—" she shrugged "—it just didn't work out."

"It just didn't work out, huh? Let me guess. He wanted more and you ran away." She sucked in a deep breath and shot him a sharp look. Nicholas shrugged. "Sorry if I struck a nerve, it's just what you do to every guy who shows interest in you."

"I do not."

"Do too."

Brooke snapped her lips shut. She would not get into some juvenile argument with him. Because they both knew he was right.

Her phone rang. She lifted it to the ear that didn't have the earpiece she'd use to communicate with Nicholas should they get separated. "Hello?"

"Hi," Jonas said.

"Hi." Did she hear footsteps? "Are you pacing the floor?"

A short, humorless laugh filtered through the line. "Yes."

"Well, you can stop. Nothing's happening—" A shadow to her left caught her attention. She nudged Nicholas who nodded. He was already watching him, tracking him with his eyes. The dark SUV blended into the nighttime surroundings. If they opened the doors, the interior lights would stay off. Even her cell phone was on the dimmest setting. There was no way the guy now approaching the back of Jonas's house would know they were watching him. "Gotta go. Someone showed up. I'll call you in a bit." She hung up on his protest and opened the passenger door. Nicholas was already approaching the house, his weapon drawn, his dog, Max, at his side.

Brooke pulled her own gun, let Mercy out of the

back and went in the opposite direction of Nicholas. She rounded the corner of the house just behind Mercy. The dog barked and made a beeline for the figure at the back door.

"Police! Freeze!" Brooke called.

Nicholas started to close the gap. "Don't move!" The man turned, raised his hands. Instead of deciding he was caught, he spun and darted for the back fence that separated Jonas's house from the neighbor behind him. The dark-clad figure scaled the fence and dropped to the other side. Nicholas went after him. Brooke called to Mercy and together, she and the dog went another route.

Back around the side of the house, Brooke was just in time to see the would-be intruder bolt down the street. Nicholas let Max go with the command to stop the fleeing fugitive, so Brooke kept Mercy beside her. Max cut loose with a low woof and loped off in pursuit, his strides long and even. Brooke lost sight of him as she and Nicholas raced to catch up. The guy was fast.

Brooke figured Max was faster.

Until she and Nicholas almost slammed into the tall chain-link fence when they turned the next corner.

She'd hung up on him. Jonas glared at the phone as though the blame lay with the device. He growled and stomped out of his temporary bedroom at the veterinary office.

Brooke had hung up on him because someone was near his house and probably trying to break in. Their surveillance plan worked, but would she be in danger now? He paced to the door. Two officers sat in the parking lot. He knew another one was parked at the back.

And one was at the Fuller household where Felix was spending the night.

Not that he expected that someone would be able to figure out where Felix was if they were looking for him, but he had to admit knowing an officer was watching out for his son made him feel better. He and Brooke had discussed picking Felix up and bringing him back to the office for the night, but they decided not to. Brooke argued that he was probably safer where he was at this point. It wasn't the Fuller house that had been bombed or the Fuller house that had been broken into. They'd come looking for the phone, not Felix.

He appreciated the fact that no one was taking any chances with his safety, but now Brooke might be in danger.

But that was her job. She was probably in dangerous situations all the time. That was what she did, right?

Yes, but it didn't make it any easier for him to deal with. Not when she was in danger because his son had taken a phone that didn't belong to him and the wrong people had tracked him down.

He had to know she was all right. He walked to the front desk and grabbed his keys. His car was in the first parking spot. He paused for a second. What if he went to find her and just got in the way?

But he wouldn't. He'd drive past his house and see if anything was happening, make sure everything was under control. Jonas headed out the door and walked over to the police officer who was exiting his vehicle.

"Sir? You need to go back inside."

"I'm going to run an errand." He switched directions and headed for his car, his worry pushing him and spurring him to move faster. "I'll be back shortly."

"I don't advise you leaving on your own."

"I wouldn't if it wasn't an emergency."

"Let me call it in and see if they want someone to tail you then."

"I don't have time to wait, but I'm going to my house for a few minutes. You can send someone there." He slid into the driver's seat, cranked the car and backed from the parking spot. As he pulled to a stop at the edge of the lot, he glanced in his rearview mirror to see the officer speaking into his radio and heading for his car.

He was probably going to follow him anyway, but Jonas didn't care. He wasn't going to sit around and wait for someone to figure out what to do with him.

Brooke was at his house and might be headed into danger. He couldn't just sit around twiddling his thumbs waiting to hear that she was okay.

Brooke hauled herself over the fence of the old textile office building. Backup was on the way, but there was no time to wait. The man they were chasing would be gone. And he was a link to the case. A case she very much wanted to solve. She'd beat Nicholas to the fence so he'd just have to stay with the dogs unless he could find another way in.

Her feet pounded against the crumbling asphalt parking lot. The building had been up for sale for years and each year it seemed to erode even more than the last. She caught sight of movement around the side of the building and took off after it, whispering her location to Nicholas.

She rounded the corner with caution, weapon held in front of her. Nothing. Except an open door.

Had he gone in or simply opened the door to head

around the building? She pressed her finger against the earpiece. "Are you inside the fence?"

"Just now. Had to cut my way through. You get him?"

"Not yet." She kept her voice low, her back to the side of the building.

A screech came from inside the building. Guess that answered that question. "He's inside. I think he pushed open one of the steel doors at the back. I'm going after him."

"Backup will be right behind you. Max and I are on the way."

Brooke gave him her location and slipped through the door into the dark. She stopped just inside to the right, making sure she didn't make herself a target in the open doorway. She let her eyes adjust, but she still had trouble seeing anything. Too dark. Easy for someone to sneak up behind her. She needed a light, but didn't dare take the flashlight from her belt.

The good thing was if it was dark for her, it was dark for him. As her eyes adjusted, she could make out shapes so it wasn't pitch-black. She had to be careful to stay in the shadows. Again, if she could see a little, so could he.

She moved softly, her steps cautious, her ears tuned to the area around her. Her neck and back tingled. She expected a bullet to slam into her at any moment. The vest she wore would offer some protection for her torso, but nothing for her head. She hadn't seen a weapon on the man running from Jonas's house, but until she saw otherwise, she'd treat him as armed. And dangerous.

"Where are you?" she whispered.

"Max, Mercy and I are coming inside."

She heard a scrape to her left and spun, her weapon

ready, hands steady in spite of the adrenaline pumping through her.

A light flashed then disappeared. Footsteps on stairs. The sound still coming from her left. Brooke moved toward the noise, still cautious, but determined to stop him. Shadows danced around her, light from the half moon filtering through the dirty windows. And the blue lights now flashing, offered even more light. "Up the stairs," she whispered. "To the left of the door about twenty feet." She placed her foot on the first step, then started up.

"Got it. Backup's outside."

"Saw the lights."

A loud scrape from the top of the stairs made her pause. The windows along the second floor offered very little light. She could make out shapes, but nothing moving. She took another step, which put her about halfway up the staircase.

A large shadow appeared at the top of the stairs. An object teetered on the edge of the highest step. She blinked, her brain trying to discern the image.

Then the thing wobbled once again. A head appeared around the edge. A grunt reached her ears.

Brooke finally registered what was happening and turned to flee as a loud rumble came from behind her and whatever was at the top of the step slid toward her. She gasped as her foot turned on the last step and she fell to the floor. She rolled and looked up to see a large upside-down desk a split second away from crushing her.

FOUR

Jonas's drive past his house resulted in nothing. But the police cruiser that zipped past him as he turned back on the main highway caught his attention and he followed it to the old textile office building. Police tape ran the length of the fence. The K-9s and their handlers were out and the air crackled with law enforcement energy.

He couldn't get to the fence due to all of the emergency vehicles so he parked and stood on the hood of the vehicle. He scanned the faces, looking for the one that he most wanted to see. Not there. One of the officers to his right on the other side of the fence pointed to the building and said something into his phone.

Was Brooke inside the building? Or was she just lost in the crowded chaos?

Gawkers from the nearby neighborhoods had come to the line to see what was going on and officers held them back. Jonas could go no farther either. He would have to wait. His fingers curled into fists. He forced them to relax. *Don't get anxious until you have something to be anxious about.* The order didn't work. He scanned the fence line and looked for a way in.

Hopelessness coursed through him as he realized he

was in for a wait. There was no going through and no going around.

A car pulled up beside him. The vehicle had the Capitol K-9 logo on the side. The officer climbed from the vehicle, a frown on his face. He flashed his badge at Jonas. "Are you Jonas Parker?"

"I am."

"I'm Chase Zachary. I got a call you went AWOL."

"Something like that," he muttered. "Brooke called me and had to hang up because she was on surveillance and someone showed up. I had to make sure she was okay."

"You might want to leave that to us. Now would you please get back in your vehicle? I'll follow you home."

Jonas had great respect for law enforcement, for the officers who put their lives on the line every day for him. If it had been anyone else in that building besides Brooke, he might have followed the order. Instead he shook his head. "I'm waiting right here until I know she's safe."

Chase lifted a brow. Then he narrowed his eyes and gave Jonas a closer once-over. Whatever he saw must have convinced him arguing would be futile. "She means something to you?"

"Yes." Jonas didn't feel the need to elaborate.

"Right. Then sit in my vehicle at least. We don't need some sniper trying to take you out while you wait."

Jonas blinked. "Sniper?"

"You've had two incidents tonight. A break-in and a Molotov cocktail through your window. Seems someone's after you."

Jonas nodded. Without another word, he opened the passenger door to the K-9 vehicle and climbed in. He slammed the door, his gaze on the building. "Can you get us through?"

"Of course I can. No reason to, though. It's being handled." A dog nudged his ear and without thought, Jonas reached back to scratch his ears. "Who's this?"

"Valor."

"He's beautiful." The Belgian Malinois butted up under Jonas's hand again. Jonas complied with another ear rub.

"He's a great partner."

Jonas looked at the building again. He knew the situation was being handled but that knowledge didn't stop him from wanting to be closer. "She's in there, isn't she? She went in after him."

Chase nodded. "She and Nicholas Cole, another K-9 team member. And the dogs. They'll get him. There's no way he can get out of there without someone grabbing him."

"What if he decides not to come out? What if he decides he wants to make one last stand?"

"Then it could get ugly. But Brooke and Nicholas are trained. They can handle him. They'll get him."

"Of course they will." Because if *they* didn't get him, whoever they'd chased inside might get *them* and Jonas didn't think he would survive that. *Don't let her die because of me, God, please.*

Brooke clasped Nicholas's hand and rose to her feet with a grunt. She swayed and took a moment to get her footing and catch her breath. "Thanks."

"You okay?" he asked. He looked pale and a little shaken himself.

"Yeah." She looked at the mangled pile of wood and steel. Nicholas had pulled her away at the last possible second. "How much do you think that weighs?"

"More than you want slamming on top of you." She shuddered and Nicholas patted her shoulder. "Don't think about it."

"I'm not." But she was. If he hadn't pulled her out of the way, she would be dead or seriously injured. "This guy is playing hardball," she muttered. She maneuvered around the part of the desk that blocked the stairs and started up. Nicholas stayed right with her. Barking reached her ears.

"I hear Max," Nicholas said.

"Yeah, I do, too. He's already up there?"

"I sent him up as soon as I pulled you out of the way. Mercy's just inside the door downstairs waiting like a good girl." He radioed in that they were still in pursuit. Brooke led the way down the hall, her footsteps echoing on the bare concrete that once had probably been covered in carpet.

The barking continued. "He's got someone cornered."

"Or he's trapped and can't get to the person," Brooke agreed.

Brooke and Nicholas came to the end of a hall. And a closed door. Nicholas gave the command for Max to sit and be quiet. Brooke held her weapon ready. Nicholas reached around her and opened the door. Brooke swung in. Max darted ahead and up another set of stairs. She followed him to the next level.

"Roof access door," Nicholas said.

They played the same dance and she breathed a bit easier when no gunshots came her way. Max pushed through and out onto the roof. Nose to the ground then in the air, he darted to the side of the building. And sat.

Brooke rushed over. "Fire escape."

"The guys would have seen him. Where did he go?"

He tapped into his earpiece. “Did you see him come down the north side of the building? Down the fire escape?”

Brooke heard the negative response and took in the area. She stepped out on the fire escape and tried to think like a desperately fleeing fugitive. “He didn’t go down.”

“What?”

“He went over.” She nodded to the overgrown trees lining the back of the building, just on the other side of the fence. “He grabbed that limb and shimmied down that tree. Or even crossed over to the next one. They’re so close together, he could have been three or four trees in before he climbed down.”

Nicholas shook his head. “You’ve got to be right. He never set foot on the ground or our guys would have nabbed him.”

She slapped a hand against the wall. “Which means he got away.”

And would live to come back and strike again.

Jonas breathed a sigh of relief when Brooke walked out of the building, Mercy trotting at her heels. She was a good distance away, but he’d recognize her and her dog anywhere. “Where’s the guy who tried to break in my house?”

Chase shook his head. “I’m guessing he got away. We’ll find out soon enough.”

Jonas frowned and reached for the door handle as several law enforcement vehicles spun out of the parking lot. Nicholas and Max went with them. “Where are they going?”

“The suspect may have been seen in a different location and they’re going after him,” Chase said. “Nicholas will see if Max can pick up his scent.”

For the next several minutes, Jonas watched the organized chaos. Brooke and Mercy disappeared back into the building. "Where's she going now?"

"To see if Mercy can find anything."

A short time later, Brooke and Mercy appeared once again. She moved closer to the fence. Closer to Jonas. He could finally see her clearly. "I'm going to guess by the look on her face she and Mercy didn't have much success."

Chase sighed. "I'd say that's a good guess."

"Yeah." Jonas's sigh echoed Chase's. "May I go talk to her now?"

Chase nodded. "She'll have a bit of paperwork to do for this one."

Jonas stepped out of the vehicle and walked to the edge of the fence then along the perimeter until he came to the gate. Brooke spotted him and her brow rose. She clicked to Mercy and walked toward him. "What are you doing here?"

He drank in the sight of her. Safe, whole, alive. "You hung up on me."

That brow rose higher. "Seriously?"

"Seriously. You scared me."

Brooke's jaw dangled slightly before she snapped it shut. "Sorry about that."

"I know it's your job, Brooke," he said softly. "It's just going to take a bit of getting used to when you're called into a dangerous situation."

"Getting used to?" she repeated.

He supposed that statement did make it sound like he planned to be around for a while. Then realized that was exactly what he planned. Now if he could just convince her.

Her expression softened. "I get it, but you really should have stayed put. You're going to have to trust that I can do my job. That I'm good at it and I take precautions, not risks."

He nodded. "I'll remember that."

"Good."

A man in khakis and a blue polo shirt headed toward them. He held a hand out to Brooke. "Officer Clark. You want to tell me why the Capitol K-9 Unit is involved in this one?"

Brooke shook the man's hand. "Detective David Delvecchio of the DC police department, meet Jonas Parker. It was his house the guy was trying to break into. We had a stakeout going on, but unfortunately, as you can see, he got away."

The detective eyed Jonas, then turned his gaze back on Brooke. "You want to tell me a little more?"

"Jonas's son found some evidence linking to the Rosa Gomez case, which of course is also related to the Jeffries shooting."

"I see." His eyes flicked back and forth amongst the three, Brooke, Chase and Jonas. He finally settled back on Brooke. "How did he get away from you?"

She rubbed her forehead. "He went out onto the fire escape on the second floor, jumped into one of the large trees across the fence line and climbed down. At least that's what we think."

"So it's time to expand the search." Chase finally broke his silence.

"Yes."

Jonas pulled his keys from his pocket. "I guess I'll head back home…er…to my office, I mean."

"I'll take you to your car then follow you," Brooke said.

Chase nodded. "I'm going to check in with Gavin and Nicholas and see what I can do to help."

Detective Delvecchio nodded. "I'll fill my officers in. Keep me updated, will you?"

"Of course," Brooke said.

Brooke said her goodbyes and motioned for Jonas to go ahead of her. She'd parked not too far from his own vehicle, just outside the fence. He turned to her. "I'm glad you're all right."

"I'm sorry you were worried."

He shrugged. "Maybe it was stupid of me to come out here, but I just couldn't sit at the office. I'm the one who should be sorry."

"It wasn't exactly smart after the fact there have been two violent incidents against you tonight, but I get it."

"So you're not mad?"

"No. I'm frustrated. I wanted to catch that guy."

He nodded. "I wanted you to catch him, too."

She patted his arm. "It's not over yet."

He had a feeling truer words were never spoken. "Meaning he'll be back?"

She drew in a deep breath and let it out slowly. "Probably."

Sunday morning, Jonas slipped from the cot he'd spent the past couple of hours tossing and turning on. It wasn't the cot's fault. It was actually pretty comfortable. He just couldn't shut his mind off. He stepped into the bathroom and looked into the mirror, gave a grimace and averted his eyes. He'd definitely had better mornings.

In the early days of his divorce, he'd often slept at his office. He'd finally had the bathroom installed when things had lagged in the courts and he'd gotten tired of showering at the YMCA. When the dust had settled she'd gotten the house, he'd gotten five-year-old Felix, and his practice. And Jonas was fine with that.

He'd purchased the house he and Felix lived in now and they'd made a good life together. At least he'd thought so. Over the past several years, each time he ran into Brooke stirred his restlessness, though. She made him long for things he'd thought he'd left in the past. Things he'd refused to allow himself to hope for.

Now he found himself looking forward to the day simply because he was going to see Brooke again. The only thing that marred that sweet anticipation was the fact that someone had bombed his house last night. Okay, that and the fact that Felix was still having issues no matter how hard Jonas tried to help him. If it wasn't a fight, it was grades.

He sighed and mentally recited his to-do list. Call his home owners insurance company was number two. Find out where Felix had gotten the phone was definitely number one.

And learning if anyone had managed to capture the guy who'd returned to his house last night. Brooke had followed him to his office, and they'd planned their next move. Get Felix from his friend's house and find out where he got the phone. Usually, he and Felix attended the local community church. He wasn't that active, but he couldn't seem to completely tear himself away from his faith. In fact, at this point in his life, he knew he should be reaching out for it with both hands. So today would be a different kind of Sunday. He paused. "I guess I should be mending my fences with You, shouldn't I, God?"

Silence echoed through the bathroom and Jonas sighed

and went back to his morning routine. Maybe God was tired of listening.

He'd just finished brushing his teeth when he heard his assistant arrive. Then voices reached him. He stepped into the lobby to find Claire Simpson and Brooke introducing themselves. Brooke hadn't wasted any time getting back to his office this morning. "Good morning," he said.

Brooke nodded. "Morning."

"I see you two have met."

Claire nodded. "I was just telling her what a beautiful dog she has."

"Claire loves anything with four legs," he told Brooke. "Let me just leave a few instructions for her and we'll head out."

He could see the curiosity in Claire's narrowed eyes, but didn't want to take time to explain Brooke's presence in addition to the other things he needed to tell her. He glanced at the clock on the wall. Eight forty-five. He'd told the Fullers he'd pick up Felix at nine-thirty. Plenty of time to cover the morning's work with Claire. He looked at Brooke. "You get any sleep?"

She shook her head. "Not much. I finished the paperwork and closed my eyes for a few minutes."

Jonas rubbed a hand down his freshly shaven chin. "I can't believe you were right. The whole smoke bomb thing was just to get us out of my house so someone could search the place."

"It looks like it."

"Should have set it up so an officer was inside my house and could have just grabbed the guy when he broke in."

"Maybe." She gave him a soft lopsided smile. "Mercy

and I'll be in the car," Brooke said. "Nice to meet you, Claire."

"You, too, Brooke."

They left and within minutes Jonas had finished up with Claire and was climbing into the passenger seat. Mercy sat in the back in her special kennel. "So tell me more about who Felix spent the night with?"

Her question grounded him, brought all of his worries surging to the surface. "He's a friend from school and the track team. His name is Travis Fuller." He gave her the address, and she entered it into the GPS and pulled out of the parking lot. "I can tell you how to get there," he said, amused.

"I don't want to have to worry about it. You said Felix had been getting into trouble."

Jonas sighed. "Yes." He shook his head. "He's been getting in fights lately. His grades are circling the drain, and his attitude is getting hard to tolerate." His hand fisted on his thigh. "I'm up to my ears trying to keep my practice going since my partner quit three months ago."

"Working a lot of hours?"

"Too many," he admitted.

"And Felix is taking advantage of your distraction."

"In a big way. I know it, I see it, but I feel trapped. I can't ignore my work or I won't be able to keep a roof over our heads, but I can't ignore Felix either or I'm going to be visiting him in juvenile detention." He didn't know why he was baring his soul to her, but he had to say it felt good to share it.

"I'm sure you do the best you can. It can't be easy being a single parent."

"It stinks." He gave a soft laugh. "But I love that kid more than anything."

"Yeah," she whispered. "I can tell."

He reached over and snagged her hand to squeeze her fingers. His throat tightened. "I've missed you, Brooke."

She sucked in a deep breath and shot him a glance out of the corner of her eye. "I've missed you, too."

He blinked and she laughed. "What? You didn't expect me to admit it?"

"No."

She shook her head. "The past is sitting like a weight between us, isn't it?"

"Yes."

She tapped the wheel and made a left turn. "I don't know what to tell you, Jonas. I thought I was making the right decision at the time when I chose to keep all distractions to a minimum and focus on my career."

"So it was strictly your career that was keeping you from being willing to talk about us having a future together?"

"It was part of it."

"What was the other part?"

A sigh slipped from her and she gave a small shrug, but didn't answer the question. He relished the fact that she hadn't pulled her hand from his yet and continued to watch her as she drove. "I thought we had something, that we could have been good together. I never did understand why you wouldn't give me a chance. As you can imagine, all kinds of things ran through my mind. Was it because I was divorced? Because I had Felix?"

She seemed to think about it. Then slipped her fingers from his. He grimaced. He wanted to kick himself. He'd moved too fast. Too much too soon. She'd been back in his life for just a few hours and he was already scaring her away.

But this time she didn't run. "No, your divorce didn't have anything to do with it. And Felix is a precious gift. He never factored into why—" She fell quiet and he hoped she'd elaborate. She didn't. "When we were friends," she said, "you never really talked about your ex-wife. I mean never. Like not one word. And when I brought her up, you changed the subject. Mostly to talk about Felix."

"Really?"

"Yes."

He thought about that. Was she right? Maybe. "What do you want to know about her?"

She shrugged. "What happened with you two? Why did you split up? Or is that too personal?" she asked.

"Not too personal. It's not a secret. She had a problem with commitment."

"Ah."

"She found someone else who suited her 'live and let live' lifestyle better than I did." He shrugged.

"What? So she left you? Why would she leave *you*? Is she *crazy*?"

Jonas barked a short laugh. "Well, those questions just did more for my self-esteem than anything else I could think of."

She flushed and it endeared her to him. She also looked uncomfortable. He let her off the hook. "I miss what could have been, but I don't miss her now."

"But Felix does?"

He sighed. "No, he doesn't remember her. He misses the idea of her."

"He wants a mother."

"He does, but when she left us, she left. Like I have no idea where she is or what she's doing now."

"You've had no contact with her at all?"

"None. After I signed the papers, she disappeared from our lives."

Brooke pulled to the curb of the Fuller home and cut the engine. "I'm really sorry about that."

"I was too at the time. But it is what it is and I've moved on." He looked at the house. "And now I'm ready to get some answers from my son."

"You want me to go with you?"

"No. I'll get him. I don't want to say anything in front of his friend."

"I'll wait here."

He nodded and climbed from the car. He walked toward the front door and drew in a deep breath. Trouble and Brooke had re-entered his life without any warning. He prayed the trouble was resolved fast and left as quickly as it appeared.

He just hoped Brooke didn't go with it.

FIVE

Brooke watched him walk up to the front door and ring the bell. She admired his broad shoulders and strong back. He'd always kept himself in great physical condition, and that hadn't changed. His love of all things sports kept him fit.

She glanced in the rearview mirror, wondering who'd thrown the bomb in Jonas's house last night. Who had they chased and lost? She'd never had a glimpse of his face. His dark clothes disguised his build, and the baseball cap had hidden his features. The darkness had definitely worked in his favor.

A young teen stepped outside onto the front porch. He had a black backpack slung over his right shoulder. Brooke would have known he was Jonas's son had she spotted him in a crowd. A miniature replica of his father, he had sandy blond hair and a lanky build. She'd seen him as a young child about five years old and he was now just an older version of the child she remembered. She knew that he had Jonas's light brown eyes, too.

The sullen expression was all his own, though.

He shoved past Jonas then lifted his head and saw her sitting behind the wheel. He stopped, his frown deepening. He turned and said something to Jonas, who nodded. Jonas shook hands with the man still standing in the doorway then the two of them headed toward the car.

Jonas slipped into the passenger seat. His son slumped in the back next to Mercy's kennel.

Brooke took a deep breath and let it out in a slow silent whoosh. She caught Felix's eye in the mirror and he looked away. "Hi," she said. "I'm Brooke."

"Hi," he mumbled.

He didn't ask who she was or seem to care that she was there. "You hungry?"

He perked up at that question. "Yeah, I didn't have time to eat breakfast." He shot his dad an accusing look.

"Hey, it's nine-thirty. You had plenty of time to eat."

"I'm a teenager, Dad. I sleep in on Sunday morning. Or I do when I'm spending the night with a friend and we plan to get breakfast at church."

"The whole breakfast thing might be my fault, I'm afraid," Brooke said. "I insisted on getting you early. Hence the offer to feed you."

"Oh." The defiant look fell away and he actually gave her a curious look. "Okay. Sure. Where are we going?"

"What's your favorite breakfast place?"

"The Original Pancake House on M. Lee Highway." He and Jonas spoke at the same time and she smiled.

"Sounds good to me." She glanced in the rearview mirror and waited for the dark vehicle coming up beside her to pass. It slowed and she tensed, her mind flashing to the night before, her hand moving to her weapon. When the car passed, she let out a slow breath. Not everyone is after him, she reminded herself. But someone was and she'd take all precautions to make sure Jonas—and now Felix—stayed safe.

She pressed the gas and pulled away from the curb. Fifteen minutes later after several failed attempts at conversation with Felix, she parked and they climbed from the vehicle, Mercy trotting obediently at her side.

Once seated with Mercy at Brooke's feet under the table, they ordered and silence fell again. Jonas caught her gaze. She nodded. He cleared his throat. "Felix, someone broke into our house last night."

The teen's head shot up and for the first time that day, he met his father's gaze. "What? Why? Are you okay? Did they catch him?"

"Yes, I'm fine, thanks." Jonas's jaw worked. She could see he was touched at his son's concern. "The house isn't so fine, but we are." He explained what happened and that they would have to stay at his office until the insurance company could give an appraisal on the damage. "But I've got friends in high places. We'll get it taken care of pretty fast."

Felix looked dazed. "So who are you again?" he asked her. Finally something other than defiance on his face.

"I'm Brooke Clark. I work for a law enforcement organization called the Capitol K-9 Unit." Felix's eyes flicked toward Mercy, who sat under the table, her head the only part of her body poking out. Brooke answered his silent question. "Mercy and I are partners. Your dad called us last night after the break-in."

"Why you?"

"I found this." Jonas pulled the phone from his pocket and slid it across the table.

Felix's eyes went wide, and he clamped his lips together.

Brooke's senses tingled. "Where did you get it?" she asked him.

Felix crossed his arms and looked away, the defiance back in spades. Jonas gave a huff of frustration. "Tell me, Felix. This is important. A picture of a dead woman is on this phone, and we need to know what you know."

Felix swallowed and a flash of fear crossed his face, but he refused to comment. Jonas's face began to darken, and his eyes turned thunderous. Brooke laid a hand on his arm. He sat back, and she could tell he was putting good effort into gaining control of his temper. "Felix, do you mind if I tell you a story?"

He jerked and shot her a confused look. "About?"

"About a little boy who no longer has a mother."

Felix's fist tightened around his glass and for a moment Brooke wondered if he was going to pick it up and throw it. "Sure," he gritted. "What about him?"

"About two months ago, a woman named Rosa Gomez was killed. Even though it hasn't been proved to be murder yet, we believe she was pushed off the cliffs at President's Park. She had a little boy who's only two years old. The good thing is that Rosa had a sister named Lana. Lana now has custody of little Juan, but losing his mother shouldn't have happened. We want to catch the person who took her away from him."

Felix flicked a glance at his father. "He doesn't have a dad either?"

"Not one that wants to be in the picture," Brooke said. "At least that's the impression we've gotten so far since no one has come forward to say he's the father."

Felix took a swig of his drink, then set the glass back on the table with a thunk. The waitress delivered the food and a lull rose. Jonas thanked the woman, who nodded and left.

"Do you mind if I say the blessing?" Brooke asked.

"No, go ahead," Jonas said. Felix looked a little uncomfortable, but didn't protest.

Brooke prayed over the food and asked God to continue to keep them safe. They ate in silence for the next few minutes. "What's going to happen to him, to Juan?" Felix asked.

"Right now, he's with his aunt, so he's being taken care of, but his mom is gone and we want to find who killed her so he doesn't have to grow up wondering." Felix looked ready to burst into tears, but Brooke hoped her words would get the boy to tell them what he knew. She didn't like being so manipulative, but every word she spoke was true. "We've tracked down every lead we could get, but lately, it seems the trail has grown cold. Until now. Until your dad called to tell me about the phone. This is a huge deal for us, Felix. Would you please tell us what you know about the phone?"

"I found it," he blurted. "On the cliffs, buried under the rocks near the police tape. I didn't know it belonged to a dead woman. I didn't know, I didn't."

"Okay. I believe you." Brooke felt Jonas tense beside her. She spoke quickly before he had a chance to interrupt. "Would you be willing to show us where you found it?"

"Yes. I'll show you." Now that Felix had confessed, he couldn't seem to get the words out fast enough. "I didn't mean to steal it. I thought someone had just lost it. I knew once I got it charged, I could connect to the internet to play games with my friends. That's all I wanted it for."

"How'd you get—and keep—the battery charged?" Jonas asked.

He shrugged and looked down at the table. "I couldn't charge it until the day before yesterday. Travis finally found an extra charger and brought it to school for me." He lifted his head and jutted his chin. "If you'd let me have a cool phone like all the other kids, I wouldn't have felt the need to keep the one I found."

"So this is my fault, huh?" Jonas asked, the thread of anger back in his voice.

Felix swallowed and offered another shrug.

Brooke's heart ached at the tension between the two. They needed each other, they just didn't know what to do about it. "Okay, here's the plan—"

"He chased me," Felix muttered.

"What?" Jonas asked sharply.

"When I found the phone," Felix said, "there was a man out there. He, uh, saw me, I guess, and chased me."

Jonas leaned in. "Who was it?"

Felix lifted a shoulder. "How should I know? Some old dude. Like about your age, I guess." Brooke barely managed to smother her snort of laughter at the look of consternation on Jonas's face at his son's comment. She looked away and processed Felix's words. But he wasn't finished. "I thought he was a cop and if he caught me he'd put me in juvie or something for being behind the crime scene tape. I ran fast and hid. He looked for me for a while, but I was faster and smarter."

"Good for you," Brooke said. "I'm glad he didn't catch you. He could have been a dangerous guy."

Felix shivered. "I didn't think about him being dangerous, I just didn't want him to catch me."

"When did you find the phone?" Jonas asked.

"A couple of months ago."

Brooke glanced at Jonas, her mind spinning with possibilities. Sometimes deduction was a "what-if" game. "Okay, so you found the phone a couple of months ago.

You get it charged up day before yesterday. Felix, last night the person who broke into your house demanded your dad give him 'the phone.'"

Felix flinched. His gaze jumped from his father to Brooke then back to Jonas. "Are you sure you're really okay?"

"I'm fine, but I don't think the timing is a coincidence."

"I don't either," Brooke said.

Jonas rubbed his eyes. "You think whoever is after the phone has just been waiting for it to come back online?"

"I do." She nodded and took the last bite of her food.

"And tracked it via the GPS."

"Exactly." She nodded to the phone. "I can't believe the thing still works. I mean, you didn't find it the day she died, did you?"

"I don't think so. I remember that it had rained that day. I was throwing rocks into the puddles to see how high the water would go. There was a big puddle behind the police tape, so I ducked under. I moved one of the rocks and found her phone." He shrugged. "It had a Life-Proof case on it," Felix said. Brooke nodded. The case would have protected it against the elements. "The battery was dead when I found it," Felix said. "I took the case off to make it easier to play the games once I got it charged. I didn't know someone would be tracking it." He dipped his head and studied his fingers. "I guess I should have turned it in to someone when I found it, huh?"

Jonas sighed. "Yes, you should have, but there's nothing to be done about that now. The important thing is that you're telling the truth now."

Brooke drew in a deep breath. "Absolutely. Thanks for telling us this, Felix. I appreciate it."

"I'm sorry," he said, his voice low, eyes on the table once again.

Jonas reached across the table to cover his son's hand when the window over the booth behind them ruptured.

SIX

Jonas registered the bullets riddling the side of the restaurant, the glass falling, the screams surrounding him. All he could do was wrap one hand around Felix's wrist and the other around Brooke's arm and yank them to the floor.

He covered Felix with his body as best he could while he scrambled to think, to picture a way out. What if they came inside? Terror slammed through him. He had to keep Felix safe. He stayed still, feeling Felix's heartbeat slam against his own. "Be still, don't move," he yelled above the screams, the chaos.

The roar of an engine, then the squeal of tires spinning against the asphalt reached his ears.

Were they gone? He stayed put for another few seconds, waiting, listening. When nothing more happened, Jonas lifted himself away from his son. He ran his shaking hands over Felix's face, his arms, chest, checking for blood. And found nothing. Felix stared at him, freckles looking 3-D against his white face. "Are you hurt?" Jonas asked him.

"No." Felix blinked. "I don't think so."

Jonas turned. "Brooke? You okay?"

"Fine." Her fingers trembled, but she pushed away from him and scrambled to her feet. She checked the dog, then glanced out the window. "He's getting away. Stay here and stay down! I'm going to see if I can get a plate." She and Mercy bolted through the restaurant. Jonas grabbed Felix to him and held him as he searched the restaurant for anyone with injuries. Sirens sounded in the distance.

Was the shooter really gone? Had they just lived through a drive-by?

"Dad?"

His son's shaking voice cracked.

"Yeah?"

"Are you okay?"

"I'm okay." He pulled Felix to him for a hug, and the teen didn't resist. He held him for a brief moment and then the chaos escalated a notch with the arrival of law enforcement.

Brooke came back in, her face tense, jaw set. She probably didn't get a plate. She beelined for them as more cops and paramedics swarmed the restaurant. Brooke must have told them it was all clear. Which meant the shooter got away. Brooke motioned for them to follow her. Jonas gripped Felix's arm and led him away from the scene. The noise level rivaled that of a jet plane. Once outside, Brooke turned to say something and stopped. Her eyes went wide. "You *are* hurt."

"What?" Felix frowned.

"Who?" Jonas asked.

"You." She reached for his arm. He looked down to find it bleeding. The low throb of pain finally registered with him.

"It's just a scratch."

"We'll let the paramedics make that diagnosis. Come on over here."

"I'm a doctor, remember?"

Felix snorted. "You're a vet, Dad. Let a real doctor look at it."

"Thanks so much, son. Nothing like keeping a person humble," he muttered. But he saw the worry in Felix's eyes and nodded. "Fine, if it will make you two feel better."

Brooke led him over to one of the ambulances. While the paramedic patched him up stating, "It's only a scratch, you're a fortunate guy," Brooke and Mercy dove into the fray of the investigation. He watched her put Mercy to work, the dog sniffing, looking for any evidence that might help them discover who had just shot up the restaurant.

And why.

Jonas decided not to let denial take over. There was no doubt in his mind that this shooting was related to the other two incidents from last night. What scared him was that whoever was after the phone didn't seem to care if he hurt someone else in the process to get it. Innocent people could have been seriously injured or killed in this latest episode and that scared Jonas to the bone.

Mercy didn't seem to find anything to interest her. The crime scene unit moved in and an officer approached him. "Do you feel up to giving your statement?"

"Sure." His arm throbbed, but he'd refused the painkiller offered. He needed a clear head. His glance slid back to Brooke and he watched her nod at one of the other Capitol K-9 Unit members as she walked toward him. She'd called for reinforcements.

Which meant she'd come to the same conclusion he

had. Everything was related. He just hoped they managed to live long enough to figure out the connections.

Brooke tried to rub the grit from her eyes. She was used to going with very little sleep sometimes, but that didn't mean she liked it. She walked over to fellow team member Nicholas Cole. A former navy SEAL, he stood tall, military written all over him. He'd left his K-9, Max, in his vehicle but she hadn't called him to the scene for Max's help. She wanted to give Nicholas the phone to pass on to Gavin, their boss. She knew the two were meeting in a couple of hours and she wasn't sure how long she'd be tied up at the scene. "Thanks for coming."

"No problem." Concern knit his brow. "You sure you're all right?"

"Shaken, but I'm fine. Grateful to be alive."

"Was anyone hurt?"

"A few scrapes and cuts, but fortunately no one was killed. The bullets hit the window of an empty booth just behind where we were sitting. I tried to get out fast enough to see a license plate, but I was too slow." Frustration at her failure bit at her.

He shook his blond head and focused pale brown eyes on her. "What's going on?"

Brooke pulled the phone from her pocket and handed it to him. "Do you have a charger in your car? I have a different kind of phone so mine won't work."

He looked at the bottom of the phone. "Yep, mine will work. Come on."

Brooke followed him with a glance over her shoulder. Jonas appeared to be finished with the paramedics. He caught her gaze and motioned for Felix to follow him. The two headed her way. She turned back to Nicholas.

"What's on it?" he asked.

"Rosa Gomez's picture."

He shot her a sharp look. "Where did you get it?"

She gave him the short version of the story. He plugged it in and the phone beeped to indicate it was charging.

Jonas and Felix drew closer. "They're escalating," she murmured to Nicholas.

"What do you mean?"

"The smoke bomb was meant to get us out of the house maybe." She nodded toward the mangled restaurant. "This was different. This was meant to kill."

Jonas stepped up beside her, and she shut off that thread of conversation. Felix hung close to his dad, still looking pale and shaken. She nodded at Jonas's arm. "Are you okay?"

His lips quirked, but his eyes remained serious. "It's just a scratch."

She smiled. "This is Nicholas. Nicholas, meet Jonas Parker and his son, Felix. Felix is the one who found the phone and was gracious enough to tell us everything he knew about it."

Felix's brows shot up and Brooke winked at him. His shoulders relaxed a fraction and he shot her a grateful look.

The two men shook hands and Nicholas gave Felix a fist bump. "Good job, kid."

"But I—" Felix started. Brooke held his gaze and he finally shrugged. "You're welcome, I guess." He swallowed. "I have the case at home if you want it, too."

"We do, thanks." Nicholas powered up the phone and gave a low whistle when the screensaver appeared. "That's her and that's her son, Juan."

Nicholas scrolled through the other pictures. "Most of them are of the boy."

Brooke leaned in. "Wait a minute, scroll back. What's the last picture she took?"

Nicholas went back to it. "This one? It's fuzzy, but it's a man."

"And they're out on the cliffs. See the outline?" Brooke pointed.

"Yes. And the date is the day she was found dead."

Brooke met his gaze. "I think it's possible Rosa took a picture of her murderer."

"It hasn't been proven to be murder," Nicholas reminded her. "It could have been an accident. This guy could be anyone."

"True," Brooke agreed, "but the fact that her wallet is still missing…"

"Could be someone have found it like Felix here found the phone."

"Okay, that's possible." Brooke pursed her lips. "But she's still connected to the Jeffries home where there was a murder. And then there was all that trouble at the children's home after it was discovered one of the children may have seen the murder…" Several weeks ago, the All Our Kids foster home had been targeted. The children and staff had been moved to a secure location until authorities were sure they were safe. Unfortunately, they wouldn't be until they discovered which child had snuck out during the night and witnessed Michael Jeffries's murder and the congressman's shooting. None of the kids would admit to being near the Jeffries home.

"You don't believe Rosa's death was an accident, do you?" Jonas asked.

"No. Not for a second. Do you?"

"No," Nicholas said. "I've made no secret that I think it's homicide. We need to keep digging for the evidence to prove she was murdered."

Brooke pulled in a deep breath. "We also need to have a meeting with the rest of the team and figure out the best way to determine who that man in the picture is."

He pulled his phone from his pocket. "I'll set up that meeting and get this phone to Gavin. I'll text you when he gives me a time. In the meantime, quit getting shot at."

"I'll do my best."

Brooke had slept fitfully last night, worried about Jonas and his son. She worried Felix would have nightmares about the shooting. She'd also been concerned that whoever was after the phone would come back again, not realizing Jonas had turned it over to the Capitol K-9 team. She knew Gavin had arranged for a protection detail on Jonas and Felix, who were staying at the veterinarian office until his home could be aired out, but she'd been unable to put the duo's safety from her mind.

And now she worried she'd be late for the eight o'clock meeting Gavin had called to discuss the new developments in the case. Mercy lay at the foot of the bed and watched as Brooke rushed to get ready. Brooke had finally fallen asleep around four in the morning and of course she'd overslept. She clicked to Mercy and she and the dog rushed out the front door to the vehicle. Mercy hopped in the back. Brooke paused to see her neighbor, twelve-year-old Christopher Denton, swinging his wooden bat. "Nice form, kiddo!"

He grinned and gave her a salute. "I had a good teacher."

She saw the balls at his feet. "No broken windows, huh?"

"I'll do my best. I'm just hittin' grounders."

She could only hope his grounders didn't turn into fly balls. Brooke had taught him how to swing a bat and connect with a baseball about two weeks ago when she'd seen him struggling. His single mother worked two jobs so Brooke looked out for the boy when she could. "Is your mom home?"

"Yes, ma'am."

"Good deal. See you later." Brooke climbed into the SUV and slammed the door. She backed out of her drive, keeping a careful eye on the surrounding area, then headed down the street to the stop sign.

Fifteen minutes later, she walked into headquarters and bolted for the conference room. The last one to arrive, she slid into her seat and let out a slow breath. "Sorry." Mercy slipped under the table with the other K-9s. Nicholas sat to her right, Gavin stood at the head of the table next to a whiteboard. Adam Donovan, a former FBI agent, leaned forward and gave her a friendly nod.

Isaac Black smirked. "They make alarm clocks, ya know? You see, you plug them into the wall and they have these buttons where you can set the time you need to wa—"

Brooke flashed him a fake smile. "Zip it, Black." Chase Zachary, a former Secret Service agent, shot her a grin and she rolled her eyes. But she truly didn't mind the good-natured ribbing; she figured it was called for. No matter how determined she might be to be on time, something usually happened to have her running at least five minutes late.

Gavin rapped the table. "Listen up, we've got some

new developments in the Jeffries case. Brooke, you want to fill everyone in?"

Brooke took a deep breath and launched into an explanation of everything that had happened since she'd been awakened by Jonas's phone call.

She ended her narration by holding up a picture they'd printed from the phone, "And this is the picture of the man we saw on Rosa's phone. We need to find him. He's either the one who killed her or he knows something about her death."

"Anyone have any suggestions on how we want to go about looking for this guy?" Gavin asked.

"Let's get his face on the news and put some flyers up," Adam said.

"Good idea. Anyone else?"

For the next hour, they bounced around ideas and finally decided on the flyers. Chase stood. "We'll get them made up and start posting them around the area. Hopefully, someone will recognize him and call us."

Gavin looked at Nicholas. "Are you still working with Selena Barrow?"

"'Working with' might be a slight exaggeration. If that's code for listening to her expound on the fact that we haven't found her cousin yet, then yeah, I'm still working with her." Serena was employed as the White House tour director. She was also Erin Eagleton's cousin. Erin's charm had been found at the murder scene and she'd been missing ever since. Serena was convinced her cousin was in danger and often showed up at the office to request an update on the case. Nicholas seemed to be the one who ended up fielding her questions more often than not.

Nicholas leaned in. "But I can handle her. That's not what's weighing on me the most. I've been doing some more digging into the congressman's business dealings." He glanced at Gavin and Brooke could see his hesitation. She knew exactly what was going through his mind. He didn't want to say anything negative about Gavin's former mentor and yet he had information he felt the team should have.

Gavin stiffened. "Go on."

Brooke bit her lip.

"You're not going to like it, but hear me out, Gavin, all right?"

"Of course."

"I'm not a big fan of the congressman," Nicholas said. "I've made no secret of that. I respect what he's done with the children's home and how he took you under his wing. He's done some good things, I'll admit that."

"But?" Gavin raised a brow.

"But I suspect that things aren't completely aboveboard with him. I'll also admit it's more suspicion and speculation than anything. I don't have any solid proof."

Gavin placed his fists on the table and leaned toward Nicholas. "If you can't prove it, don't say it. Think long and hard before you open your mouth and slander a good man."

Nicholas met Gavin stare for stare. "It's not slander, Gavin. I'm not sharing this with anyone but the people in this room."

"Then get proof."

Nicholas sat back and crossed his arms. "Right."

Gavin held his gaze a moment longer, then looked over the very still and quiet team members. "That goes for all of you." He paused and homed back in on Nicholas and his expression eased a fraction. "You're not often wrong, Nicholas, I'll grant you that." He paused and frowned. "I just think you are in this case, so tread carefully." Gavin gathered his phone and other things and headed out of the room. The others trickled slowly behind him.

Brooke got up and Nicholas touched her arm. "Hang on a sec, would you?"

She paused. "Sure."

When it was just the two of them left in the conference room, Nicholas shut the door. "Gavin's too close to this. He doesn't want to hear anything negative about the congressman."

"Yeah, I got that."

"But I'm telling you, there's something not right about him."

"What have you found out?"

He motioned for her to sit down. She did and he sat next to her, his shoulders leaned in, face tense. "I was at the White House the other day doing some snooping. I found out that Congressman Jeffries had a young aide, Paul Harrison, who quit unexpectedly. The source I talked to said he didn't know the details, just that the guy was there one day cleaning out his desk. When my source asked him what was wrong, he wouldn't say, but he was scared."

"Scared of what?"

"That's just it, I don't know and I couldn't find out."

"Which is why you didn't tell Gavin this. Have you found the aide?"

"No, not yet. Mr. Harrison disappeared shortly after he quit working for the congressman." Nicholas clasped his hands in front of him. "This whole thing stinks, Brooke. I think the congressman is dirty. I just need help proving it."

Brooke blew out a breath and leaned back in her chair. "That's going to be quite a job."

"I know. We're close, though, so close I can almost taste it. I want to put this guy away."

"If he's guilty."

"He's guilty. I've been digging into the congressman's history and activities. Especially those close ties to Thorn Industries."

"Thorn Industries is coming up a lot lately—and it's not good stuff." She pursed her lips.

"Exactly. If he's guilty of some kind of corruption, I think that would make him extremely paranoid and nervous."

"Nervous enough to kill?" Brooke narrowed her eyes as she considered her own question.

"I don't know."

"What if Rosa knew something? Or saw something?" she pressed.

"And he had to kill her to keep her quiet?"

"Maybe."

"It's possible of course, but pure conjecture."

"Which might be pure truth. I'm also going to see if I can track down the aide whose sudden departure has me curious."

Brooke stared at him for a few seconds, then gave a reluctant nod. "Okay then. If you're right, then we're not going to need just proof, we're going to need airtight, *irrefutable* proof. Like a confession kind of irrefutable proof."

"And we're going to need to watch each other's backs. There's no telling how far he'll go to protect his name."

"If you're right, we already know how far he'll go."

Brooke pursed her lips. "All right then. Let's get those

flyers up and see if we get a hit on anyone. If we do, we can immediately see if that person has any kind of link to the congressman."

"Good idea." He glanced at the closed door. "And keep this between us, I guess. I don't want to stir up Gavin's wrath any more than I already have."

"I understand." She frowned. "It's going to be hard for him if your suspicions are proven true."

"I know, but we don't have a choice. We have a dead woman who deserves justice."

"And a single dad who has a killer after him and his son."

SEVEN

Jonas hung up with the insurance company and sighed. He looked around his office and just prayed Felix was staying out of trouble while at school today. He'd been grumpy and snappy and nothing Jonas had said or done this morning had been right. Not only that, Felix had complained his toast was dry and the cereal soggy. He'd walked out the door without a look back.

Jonas rubbed his tired eyes and glanced at the clock. It was only eight-thirty in the morning, and he had a full day scheduled. The first patient would be arriving any moment and Jonas couldn't get himself together. Yesterday had been surreal and he still wasn't sure it hadn't been just one more nightmare to add to his repertoire.

He picked up the stress reliever ball from his desk and started squeezing it. Squeeze, release, squeeze, release. He threw it across the room and watched it bounce. That helped.

Claire poked her head in the door. "Mrs. Boyd is here with Chester."

Jonas forced a smile to his lips and stood. "What is it today?"

"She thinks he ate a bowl of gummy worms her grandson left on the coffee table." Chester, the big golden who ate anything he could sink his teeth into. Whether it was meant for him or not.

Jonas shook his head and headed for the door when his cell rang. "Tell Mrs. Boyd and Chester I'll be right there." He pressed the answer button. "Hello?"

"Hi, Jonas, it's Brooke."

Just hearing her voice made his day better. "Hi. How's it going?"

"Busy. We're moving full speed ahead on trying to track down the man in the picture on Rosa Gomez's phone. We're putting flyers up all over town. Since someone tossed a smoke bomb in your house two nights ago and then shot up the restaurant yesterday, we're going to put some around those areas, too. Do you mind if I bring some to your office?"

"Of course I don't mind." He glanced at the clock. "Would you be free for lunch around noon?"

"I think I could do that."

"Good. We'll talk about where to eat when you get here."

"How was Felix this morning?"

His mood soured. "Don't ask."

"Ouch. I'm sorry. He'll come around."

"Yeah." Maybe.

"See you in a few hours." She hung up.

Jonas stared at his phone. As much as he loved his job and his patients, he knew the next three hours and fifteen minutes were going to drag by.

When Brooke finally walked in the door with Mercy trotting at her heels, Jonas smiled. Then frowned. She looked so serious, with her tight jaw and set shoulders, but he was still happy to see her. "I thought noon would never get here."

At his words, her petite frame relaxed and her blue eyes gave him a glimmer of a smile. "I felt the same way. I'm starving."

"Do you think we could eat somewhere that won't get blown up or shot at?"

Her nostrils flared at the reminder and for a moment he was sorry he'd brought it up. Then she smiled. "Sure. I have the perfect place." She handed him several flyers. "Do you mind handing these out to your clients?"

"Of course not." He placed them on the front counter. "We'll post one on the door, too."

"Great, thanks."

"So. Lunch?"

"Why don't I drive?"

Claire's attention had been bouncing back and forth between the two of them. "So, I guess I'll just stay here and man the phones while you two enjoy your meal."

Jonas froze for a second before turning to Claire. She held his gaze for a moment then laughed. "I'm kidding. Enjoy yourselves."

"Are you sure? You're welcome to come with us. I could lock up for a couple of hours."

Claire waved a hand. "It was a joke, Jonas. Go on. I've got enough here to keep me busy for a while and I want to finish it before five." She picked up the tape and grabbed one of the flyers. "And I'll put this in the window right now." The phone rang. "Or I will in a minute. Go." She answered the phone with a smile.

She really had been kidding. He shook his head. He'd never been very good at picking up vibes from women and it didn't look like his skills had improved since his wife had left.

Although, he had to admit, he picked up on Brooke's vibes pretty well. And they confused him. She seemed like she wanted to get closer to him. The look in her eye, her body language. All of that confirmed it. But then when he'd try to respond, she'd get skittish and throw up a wall that left him bruised and battered when he slammed into it.

He followed her out to her vehicle and she opened the back door for Mercy. The dog hopped in and settled herself in the special area designated just for her. Brooke slipped into the driver's seat and Jonas watched her fasten her seat belt. "So do you like burgers or chicken?" she asked.

He shrugged. "I like both."

She slid him a look. "Which one do you like today?"

"Burgers."

Brooke started the car and pulled from the parking lot. "There's a little place not too far from here. Hopefully, I'll get to finish a meal. I'm waiting to hear back from Nicholas about visiting Congressman Jeffries sometime today."

"Why him?"

"We think he may have some more information about his housekeeper's death—and his son's."

"Do you think he had something to do with either?"

Brooke pulled into the diner's lot and parked. She looked over at him. "I can't say whether he did or not. But my other team member and I feel like it wouldn't hurt to talk to him again."

Jonas nodded and stepped from the car. He looked around, trying to see if anyone had followed them. He noticed Brooke doing the same. "Do you see anything?"

"No. And I was watching while I was driving. I never saw anyone suspicious behind us."

They walked into the restaurant and Brooke led him to a corner booth that had no windows. Brooke slid in and Jonas took the seat opposite her. They ordered and then Jonas looked at her. Intently. She took a sip of water. "What is it?"

Time to start tearing down some walls. "I've just wondered about you. Running into you, seeing you occasionally only made me wonder more."

"Wonder what?"

"Do you mind if I ask you a personal question?"

She didn't answer right away. Instead, she tilted her head and met him stare for stare. Finally, she shrugged. "You can ask. I won't promise I'll answer."

"Fair enough." The waitress interrupted with the serving of their order. When she left, he looked back Brooke. "Why haven't you ever married?"

Brooke froze. Well, he'd said it was a personal question. She cleared her throat. She didn't want to lie, but she didn't want to just lay the truth out there either. She offered what she hoped was a casual shrug. "I think I'm a career girl, Jonas." She looked up and met his gaze. "I've spent the past fifteen years of my life preparing, training, learning and working. I've known exactly what I wanted to do ever since I saw an old rerun of Lassie rescuing Timmy." She smiled. "I guess I just haven't let things like romance and marriage distract me." Which was all true. It didn't mean she didn't wish things were different every once in a while, but she'd accepted that her lot in life was to be alone. No man wanted damaged goods.

"I think you were pretty tempted to be distracted way back when we first met," he teased softly.

Thank goodness the waitress chose that moment to bring their food. Brooke ignored his statement and the only thing she could think to do was to bow her head to say a short silent blessing. And plead for a change of subject. She looked up to find Jonas's eyes on her. "Well?" he asked.

"Well what?"

"Come on, Brooke, admit it. You felt something for me years ago. Why did you push me away?"

"Why are you *pushing* this now?"

He hesitated. Then sighed. "Like I said, because I've always wondered. When we first met, we hit it right off. We became best friends and then when I wanted more, you threw up a wall and took off."

"It wasn't you," she whispered.

"I know. Or at least I do now. You said it was you, but at the time all I knew was you were crazy about me, too. Your rejection threw me for a loop." He gave a short, humorless laugh. "I never would have had the guts to put myself out there and tell you how I felt if I hadn't been 100 percent sure you felt the same way. So why would you push me away?"

Her palms started to sweat. She really didn't want to have this conversation, but could tell he'd been waiting a long time to say these things. She glanced at the door, wanting to run, escape the memories, the what-might-have-beens had the car wreck never happened. Of course she might never have gone into law enforcement if not for the wreck. Then she never would have met Jonas. She swallowed, then cleared her throat. "I—"

"You broke my heart," he said softly.

Brooke winced. "I—"

He shook his head, looked at his food then back at her. "Every time we'd bump into one another, I'd want to stop you and ask you these questions. I'm sorry I'm just blurting all this out. But seeing you again has resurrected all those old feelings, and I just want to know if this time could be different."

Her phone rang, and she couldn't move. "Nothing like putting a girl on the spot," she finally said. "You never did beat around the bush, did you?"

"No, not much. Still don't." He gave a small smile as her phone rang again. "After being shot at and almost blown up these past couple of days, life has come into startling clear focus for me. Answer your phone and we'll finish this conversation after you've had a bit of time to process it." He stood and wiped his mouth. "I see a client whose Boxer is scheduled to have surgery next week. I'll be right back."

She grabbed the phone, knowing he was giving her some time to think and privacy to take her call. His thoughtfulness warmed her even while his words terrified her. For a number of reasons. Nicholas's number flashed on the screen. "Clark here." Jonas walked away, his back straight, broad shoulders hinting at his strength.

"Hey, Brooke."

"What's up?"

"We've got an appointment to talk to Congressman Jeffries in thirty minutes. Can you meet me at his house?"

"Of course. I'll leave now."

"See you there."

She hung up and caught Jonas's eye. He kept his conversation with his client brief, then moved toward her while she pulled some bills from her wallet. Most of their food sat untouched and she didn't have time to have it boxed up. It would take her every minute of the thirty allotted minutes to get to the congressman's house. "I've got to go," she said. "Do you mind riding with me and waiting in the car?" She explained the call from Nicholas.

"I'll get Claire to pick me up," he said. "You don't need me along."

"You're sure?"

"I'm sure."

"All right, thanks." She snapped her fingers, and Mercy joined her at her side. She could feel Jonas's eyes on her all the way out the door and knew their conversation wasn't over. A ball of dread settled in her stomach that had nothing to do with finding a possible murderer. She'd rather face down a killer than talk about why she would never marry. That thought alone almost stopped her in her tracks. But she kept walking and thinking. And she realized she really hadn't dealt with her anguish over her inability to have children. She drew in a shuddering breath. She didn't have time to deal with her issues. She had a killer to catch.

EIGHT

As soon as Brooke climbed into her car, Jonas's phone rang. His heart dipped when he saw the number. "Hello?"

"Dr. Parker, this is Grace Hale with Falls Church Middle School."

Grace Hale, principal and disciplinarian. "Hello, Dr. Hale." He couldn't help the resignation in his voice. "What's Felix done now?"

"We caught him skipping class."

"Skip—" Jonas closed his eyes. "All right. I guess you're going to suspend him?"

"No, I think it would be best if we didn't. His grades are suffering enough. Suspension isn't going to do anything positive for him." A principal who cared. Jonas sent up a silent thank-you. "He's going to have two days of in-school suspension where he will be closely supervised while he works on material that will get him caught up." A slight pause as though Dr. Hale were weighing her next words. "I'm also going to recommend he talk to one of our counselors here."

"I see. His mother left him—us—when he was young. He's never given up hope that she would come back. Lately I think his hope is gone and that's why the surly attitude and acting out. I think he's finally come to understand that she's not coming back. You understand?"

"I do." The woman kept her tone soft, without accusation or contention. Jonas appreciated that.

"Would you trust your child's emotional well-being with the counselor you want him to talk to?" he asked.

A slight pause. "One of them, yes."

"Then that's the one he can talk to."

"Thank you, Dr. Parker."

"Dr. Hale?"

"Yes?"

Jonas cleared his throat. "Thank you for not suspending him."

"He wasn't doing anything, just sitting in the bathroom on the floor staring at the wall. I think he's hurting."

"I think he is, too." His heart ached for his son, but he just didn't know what to do for him. Maybe the counselor would help. He cleared his throat. "At least he wasn't fighting."

"Indeed." Another pause. "I heard Felix was there when someone shot at the restaurant."

Jonas flexed his arm at the reminder. It still hurt when he moved wrong. "Yes, but we talked and he seemed to bounce back."

"Sometimes appearances can be deceiving."

Very true. "All right, he can talk to your counselor, and I'll talk to him when I see him this afternoon."

He hung up with the principal and called Claire, who agreed to pick him up. He had a caseload that he needed to focus on. And he had to figure out what to say to his son. His phone rang as he was slipping it back into his pocket. A glance at the caller ID had his black mood lifting. "Hi."

"Hey, I forgot to ask you one thing," Brooke said.

"What's that?"

"Do you think after Felix gets out of school, you and he could go with me to the cliffs and he could show us where he found the phone?"

"Ah, yes, we can do that."

She paused. "You okay?"

"Not really." He told her what happened with Felix skipping class and the principal's recommendation for a counselor.

She was silent for a brief moment. "I'm here and I need to go in, but I'll just say a counselor can help. A good one anyway."

"I know. Thanks, Brooke."

"Sure thing. Talk to you soon."

He hung up. His son needed to see a counselor. Again. Jonas sighed. He'd thought Felix had been doing better. They'd been talking and hanging out and then Christmas had come and gone and Felix had started shutting him out once again. He shook his head and as Claire pulled to the curb, Jonas decided he needed to take a serious look at praying again. He had a lot to talk to God about if God was interested in hearing about it. Jonas decided it was time to find out.

Brooke stepped out of her vehicle and told Mercy to stay put. The dog gave her a mournful look, but settled down in her kennel with a sigh. The day wasn't hot, but it wasn't cold either. She left the rear windows down and the screens up with the fans blowing so Mercy would be comfortable during her wait.

Nicholas climbed out of his matching K-9 vehicle and

did the same for Max. "Did you tell him what you wanted to talk to him about?"

"No, I didn't want to give him a reason to refuse to see us."

The congressman had agreed to meet them at his house. She supposed he didn't want to have to answer questions about their presence at the Congressional Office building, although most would probably just think they were working his son's murder.

Nicholas rapped on the door and Brooke took a good look around. The house had a classy, stately air about it. The door opened.

A young woman smiled up at them. "You must be the officers who wanted to speak to the congressman."

"Yes ma'am. Is he here?"

"I'm afraid not. He had to leave suddenly. Something about a forgotten doctor's appointment. He asked me to let you know."

Brooke sighed, frustration zipping through her. "Guess we could show up at his doctor's office."

Nicholas shook his head. "It's all right. Thank you very much."

"Of course." She shut the door and Brooke turned around to stare out across the estate. "You think he's avoiding us?"

"I don't know. We'll catch up to him eventually."

She shoved a stray piece of hair behind her ear. "You'd think if he was as interested in solving his son's murder as he says he is, he'd make himself available."

Annoyance stamped itself on her team member's handsome features and he nodded his agreement. "Do you have any other ideas?" he asked.

They headed toward their vehicles. "We've got the

flyers going up, we're still examining the phone…" She shook her head. "Any luck on finding the aide?"

"Fiona thinks she may have tracked him down in Maryland working at a gas station slash convenience store. He changed his name, but did a sloppy job of running. He even used his credit card. She had a local officer snap a picture of him to verify, but warned him not to spook the guy." He pulled the picture up on his phone and turned it so she could see the clean-cut young man in his late twenties. The next picture was of the same young man with longer, shaggy hair cleaning the glass door that led into the convenience store.

"He looks different, but it's definitely the same guy."

"That's what I think."

"That's quite a career change."

"He didn't want to be found, but doesn't have the skills to stay hidden. Like I said, he used his credit card early this morning."

"Are you going to talk to him?"

"Yes, are you up for a road trip tomorrow if I can clear it with Gavin?"

"Of course." Her phone rang. She glanced at the caller ID. "Speaking of Gavin."

His brow lifted. "Great. Maybe he's got something for us. Put it on speaker, will you?"

She did. "Hi, Gavin."

"Brooke, I know you're with Harland, but this is pretty important."

"Actually, the congressman wasn't here."

"What?" She could hear the frown in his voice.

"He decided he had a doctor's appointment at the last minute. Guess he forgot about it."

"He's been under a lot of stress, you know that." Now reproval echoed back at her.

She pursed her lips. "I know."

"He'll probably call you to reschedule."

"I hope so."

"So let me get to the reason I called. Cassie called me a few minutes ago. She said she may know which kid snuck out the night of the shooting." Cassie Danvers, the director of the All Our Kids children's home. And also Gavin's fiancée.

"Who was it?"

"Tommy Benson. He's been waking up with nightmares about a tall man with a gun."

"A tall man with a gun. Could be our shooter?"

"Could be. I think it'd be a good idea for you to go by there and talk to him."

"We've talked to him before and gotten nowhere."

"Be creative. You're a female. Maybe he'll feel more at ease talking to you since he's been living with Cassie and gotten pretty attached to her."

"And you."

"Yeah."

She smiled at the sudden gruffness in his voice. He'd definitely fallen for the kid. "All right, I'll talk to Cassie and find a good time to come by and see Tommy."

"Sounds like a plan. Keep me updated."

"Of course. One more question before we hang up."

"Yes?"

She explained the need to drive into Maryland to speak to the aide.

Gavin hesitated. "This has been a crazy case," he finally said. "You go and take Nicholas with you. When do you need to leave?"

...morrow morning?" She looked at Nicholas and he nodded. "It's just about an hour over the state line into Maryland."

Gavin gave her the green light. "Keep me updated."

She hung up and looked at Nicholas. "This is a step in the right direction. Talking to the aide and finding out who the blue mitten belongs to. That little mitten found at the scene has been bothering me since the beginning. We've suspected all along one of the children from the home snuck out and saw something. Now one of them is having nightmares about a tall man with a gun."

"Sounds promising."

"I hope so. I'm feeling slightly desperate. I'll take just about anything at this point."

"Yeah. All right." He paused, then gave a short nod. "You talk to Cassie and the kids again. I'll see what time we can leave in the morning and come by and pick you up."

"Great." She thought she might give Jonas a call and see if he had any furry friends that might like to accompany her to the children's home.

Jonas sat parked at the school, in line to pick up Felix. He'd called Claire and told her not to get Felix. Jonas wanted to pick him up himself. While he waited, he checked his email and made a few calls. In the midst of checking his messages on his home voice mail, Jonas's phone beeped at him indicating an incoming call. When he saw that it was Brooke, he switched over, his heart picking up a little bit of speed. "Hi there."

"Jonas, do you have a moment?"

"Of course. I always have time for you, Brooke." She

went silent and he wondered if he was too [illegible]
bly, then decided he didn't care. "What can I do for you?"

"I was wondering if you could get your hands on a couple of puppies."

"Mercy isn't enough?"

She gave a low chuckle. "I need to get a seven-year-old boy to trust me in record time."

"Ah, I see. One puppy would probably do it. Two would cinch it." He smiled. "I have a client whose German shepherd had a litter about five weeks ago. She's probably still got them. Want me to give her a call?"

"Absolutely. I know we were supposed to go out to the cliffs, but do you think you could get the puppies and Felix and meet me so I can take the puppies out to the foster home?"

He glanced at his watch, then at the school. "Sure. I can do that. Felix should be getting out pretty soon. Do you want me to meet you there?"

"Noooo." She drew the word out and Jonas lifted a brow.

"Okay, what's the deal?"

"You can just give me the puppies. The foster home is in a safe house until the threat to the children and Cassie is over. The location of the safe house is secret right now."

"I understand. I still want to go."

"I could take you, but I'd have to blindfold you," she joked.

"You don't trust me?"

"It's not that." She sighed and turned serious. "It's just that these kids could still be in danger. If someone finds out where they are, it could be tragic. When this case broke a couple of months ago and it came out that one of the children possibly saw something at the congressman's house, someone was desperate enough to set fire to a foster home. A *foster* home, Jonas. We just can't take any chances with their lives."

Jonas knew she was absolutely right. "I get it. So blindfold us."

She didn't speak for a moment and Jonas figured he'd caught her off guard. "Really?" she finally asked.

"Sure. I'd love to have a hand in helping the kids. Their lives have been disrupted enough already. Let Felix and me come." He cleared his throat. "It might do Felix some good, too. He hasn't exactly had a perfect life with his mom leaving, but regardless of what he thinks, he's got it pretty easy." She didn't say anything for a moment. "I hope your silence means you're thinking about it."

"Actually, I am. You just gave me an idea. Do you think Felix would be willing to help us?"

"What do you mean?"

"He's the same age as some of those kids in the home. If he comes in with the puppies, they'll swarm him. Little Tommy Benson might be more willing to talk to a thirteen-year-old than an adult."

"Felix'll do it."

"Are you sure?"

Jonas closed his eyes. Would Felix be willing or would he just have on his attitude? "No, but I'll ask him."

"Okay. While you're doing that, I'll have to call my boss and tell him what we're thinking. I'm guessing he'll be all right with it, but I still need to get his input. I'll also have to let Cassie know what's going on and clear it with her, too."

"Get permission and I'll work on Felix and the puppies."

"Please tell me you're being careful, taking extra precautions."

"I am. That's why I'm in the carpool line. No more riding the bus for Felix until this is all resolved. I think there's an officer keeping an eye on us, too."

He heard her sigh. "I hate that it's necessary, but I'm concerned about Felix being a target."

"I share that concern. I've asked the principal to keep a close eye on Felix and warned her that there might be trouble."

A slight pause then, "That was smart. You're starting to think like a cop."

Realization hit him. "You'd already called the school."

"Yes, but I'm glad you're staying on top of things."

"Where do you want us to meet you?"

"At your office. I'm on my way."

"See you soon, Brooke."

She hung up and Jonas got on his phone. He knew just who to call so he wasn't worried about getting the requested pups. He just prayed he could do it without getting shot at or blown up.

Please, God, keep us all safe.

NINE

Brooke arrived at Jonas's office. While she waited, she scanned the area, looking for anyone who shouldn't be there. Satisfied she hadn't been followed, she called Gavin and received permission to take a blindfolded Jonas and Felix out to the children's home/safe house. "Sounds like a good idea. It's worth a try anyway."

"Great. Do you want to call Cassie and let her know or do you want me to?"

"I'm more than happy to call Cassie." Gavin's voice took on a warmth every time he said the woman's name.

"I kind of thought you would be."

Gavin's low chuckle made her smile. Once they hung up, her smile drooped. Would she ever have what Cassie had with Gavin? Even Adam Donovan had managed to fall in love during the investigation, with Lana Gomez, Rosa Gomez's sister. Adam's love for Lana had lit a fire under him in regards to finding out the reasons behind Rosa's death.

But unless Brooke allowed herself to open up and trust someone about her inability to have children, the possibility of finding love was nil.

What would Jonas say if she told him? He loved his

son and she knew he would love to have more children. Eight years ago he'd told her his dream to be married with a houseful of kids. It had been during one of their last conversations before she'd shut him out completely. She shook her head and shoved the painful memories aside. Or at least she tried to. The truth was, every time she was with Jonas, she couldn't help but long for what could have been. Or what could be now. She knew he was interested in picking up where they left off, but she could tell he was a bit leery of her, too.

She figured he wasn't real keen on setting himself up for another broken heart and she couldn't blame him. She knew she was giving off conflicting signals, but didn't seem to have any control over it. But if there was going to be hope for the two of them, she'd have to overcome her insecurities and fears.

His car pulled into the parking lot and she could see Felix in the passenger seat. He actually had a smile on his face, German shepherd puppies tucked under his chin. Felix and Jonas climbed out of the car and Felix juggled his armload. Jonas's eyes met hers and he gave her a slow smile. "Thanks for this." He blinked and she thought she saw moisture before he cleared his throat and looked back at his son.

The puppies licked and squirmed but Felix kept a firm yet gentle grip on them. His gaze met hers and his smile faltered. Then one of the puppies nipped his nose and he yelped, sounding a lot like his new friends. Brooke laughed and motioned for them to get in her vehicle. Mercy sat in the backseat in her kennel, her interest in the puppies clear yet controlled. Jonas opened the back door for Felix and he settled himself in. "Here's their box," Jonas said as he passed the cardboard through the door.

"I can hold them," Felix said.

"That's fine, just put your seat belt on, okay?"

The teen placed the puppies in the box while he fastened his seat belt. Brooke opened the kennel door and let Mercy investigate. The dog took her time sniffing and examining the squirmy canines. She gave them both a lick and settled back into her kennel, satisfied. Brooke shut the door and climbed behind the wheel. She started the car and pulled away, heading for traffic.

"Did your dad tell you what we need you to do, Felix?" she asked.

"He said you wanted me to use the puppies to get the kid to talk about what he saw the night that lawyer was killed."

"Right."

"But use some tact, will you?" Jonas asked. "Don't mention that night unless Brooke motions for you to say something. She's the one who's going to be asking the questions, okay?" Jonas asked.

"We already went over this. I'm not stupid, Dad."

"I know you're not, son." Jonas's sigh was heavy.

"I'm going to be close by," Brooke said, "so if I start talking, you kind of just focus on the puppies, all right?"

"I got it," Felix huffed. But Brooke could tell his attitude wasn't quite as hard as the first time she'd seen him. He fell silent during the short drive to the edge of town.

She pulled over to the side of the road. "Can you open the glove compartment and pull out those two blindfolds?"

Jonas did as she asked and passed one back to Felix.

"Seriously?" he asked.

"Seriously," Brooke said.

The boy shook his head but didn't argue, just slipped it over his eyes. "So this is kind of like undercover work, isn't it?"

He wanted to sound bored, but she caught the thread of excitement in his tone. She smiled. "Yes, it is. You're going to go in, get Tommy's trust and help us get information. All you have to do is work with the puppies."

Felix sighed and she figured they were repeating themselves a bit much. She just didn't want anything to go wrong or for the whole plan to backfire and alienate Tommy instead of getting him to talk.

"Sorry, Felix," she said softly.

"Thanks," he said just as soft.

Jonas reached over and curled his left hand around her right. And she let him.

Until she noticed the vehicle staying steady just behind them. She snagged her phone and dialed Gavin. "I need some backup."

Jonas whipped off his blindfold. "What is it?"

"Behind us. No one followed me to your office, I'm sure of it."

"Maybe it wasn't you."

"What do you mean?"

"I mean what if someone followed me from Felix's school?"

He had a point. "I think it's time we got you and Felix some twenty-four-hour protection."

"What?" Felix blurted from the backseat. "No way. I don't want someone following me around all day. It's bad enough the school resource officer won't let me out of his sight and now you want to make it a full-time thing? No way. Dad, tell her no."

Brooke ignored Felix. She understood his concern, but right now, she was growing more anxious by the second as the car behind her closed the distance.

Jonas could see Brooke's worry as her gaze snapped back and forth between the road and the rearview mirror. "Is help on the way?"

"Yes, but we may have to take care of things ourselves until it gets here."

"Take care of things how?"

"Hold on tight," she muttered. The car sped up. "He's going to try to run us off the road."

Jonas's adrenaline shot to maximum levels as he turned in the seat to catch Felix's frightened gaze. "Hang on, son." Felix nodded and held his precious cargo.

Jonas tried to get a glimpse of the driver, but the man had a mask on. The car crept closer. Closer. Jonas held his breath and gripped the door. He wanted to throw himself into the back and cover Felix with his body, but there wasn't room—or time.

And then the car following them tapped the rear bumper. The only reason they didn't spin out was because Brooke surged ahead.

"Grab something and hold on tight," Brooke shouted. She slammed the brake and spun the wheel. The car's back end swung out. Felix yelled and puppies yelped. The vehicle on their bumper flew past. Jonas caught a glimpse of it, then spinning trees.

Then they were stopped. An abrupt halt that jerked him against the seat belt. "Felix? You all right?"

The boy didn't answer. Jonas whipped his head around to see his son hovering over the two puppies. Mercy had been knocked around, but stood and shook herself. "Felix?"

Felix looked up and Jonas flinched at the blazing anger in the teen's eyes. "I'm fine. Who is doing this? And why?"

"Hold that thought," Brooke said. "They're coming back."

"What?"

Sirens sounded and the black sedan slammed on brakes before reaching their vehicle, backed up and did a one-eighty turn. It sped off and Brooke sucked in a deep breath.

Nicholas pulled up beside her. Two other police cars swept past them and gave chase. She rolled her window down. "Pretty fancy driving there," he said.

"Maybe. I'm glad you showed up when you did."

"Did you get a plate?" Nicholas asked.

"No. I tried, but couldn't catch it."

"I think I caught the letter *X* and maybe the number 3," Jonas said.

Brooke looked at him, admiration glinting in her eyes. "Nice job."

He shrugged and glanced back at Felix. He'd released the puppies back into their box and sat with his arms crossed, the glare in his eyes not having lessened. "What is it, son?"

"They can't get away with this."

"They're not," Brooke said, her tone grim. "That's why we're doing everything we can to stop them." She sighed and rubbed her forehead. "All right, let me call Cassie and tell her we're going to have to do this another day—"

"What? Why?" Felix demanded.

Jonas frowned at the boy's tone, but Brooke lifted a

brow. "You don't want to go home and chill out a little? You got knocked around a bit."

"I'm not hurt and in case you forgot, my home is a veterinarian's office right now, thanks to these people. And no, I'm not interested in chilling out. I want to find the dude that ran us off the road and tried to shoot us at the restaurant. If we don't find him fast, these things are just going to keep happening. We need to help so those kids can go back to living in their home and feel safe."

Jonas couldn't help his sagging jaw. This was his son? His surly, attitudinal teen who only thought about himself most of the time? He shot a look at Brooke, who looked more amused than anything. She gave a slow nod. "All right then. You're on. Let's get going." She looked at Nicholas. "Will you make sure we're not followed?"

"Absolutely. Officers are in pursuit as we speak."

"Good. Call me if you need anything else."

He nodded. "I talked to Jeffries and rescheduled our meeting. We're on for tomorrow morning first thing. At his house again."

She lifted a brow. "Is he going to be there this time?"

"He says he is."

Jonas watched the two converse and wondered if there was anything between them besides work. At first, jealousy flared, but then faded. He didn't get that from them. He got a sense of deep respect and friendship, but nothing more. He wanted to disregard the relief flowing through him, but couldn't. He also couldn't ignore the fact that Brooke was important to him. And the more he was around her, the more that grew. He wanted to find out if they had a chance this time around but was leery about getting his heart trampled on again.

She looked at him. "Blindfold, please."

"Seriously?" Felix asked from the back even as he did as asked without hesitation.

"Seriously."

TEN

Brooke glanced at Felix in the back and noted he still wore his half angry, half determined expression. Below the blindfold, his jaw jutted. As he grew, he would look more and more like Jonas. Not a bad thing in her opinion.

Jonas reached over and grasped her fingers once again and she let him. She needed the human contact, the reassurance that they'd survived yet another attempt on their lives.

He held her hand until she turned onto the mile-long drive that would lead to the safe house. Guard dogs patrolled the area and she had to show her ID at three different stops along the way. Finally, they reached the gate. A tall fence surrounded the property and she hoped the kids didn't have to stay there too much longer. They needed to be back in their original location near the Jeffries mansion in Flag Heights. For some of them, it was the only home they'd ever known. "You can take your blindfold off now."

"Wow, what is this place?" Felix had his blindfold off and his eyes bounced from one end of the complex to the other.

"The children's home," she said. "Are you ready to meet some people?"

"Yes." He still had determination stamped on his face, but now there was excitement present. He glanced at her. "Is the boy you told me about here?"

"The one that lost his mom?"

"Yes."

She shook her head. "No. He was for a little while, but then his aunt Lana was granted custody of him."

Felix pressed his lips together and took another look around as she parked. "Oh. I'm glad he has a mom again."

"Yeah, me, too," she said, wondering what was going through his young mind.

"My mom took off."

Jonas inhaled, but didn't say anything.

"I know," Brooke said. "I'm sure that hurts."

"Sometimes." He shrugged then nodded. "But I'm over her. It was her choice and if that's the kind of person she is, I'm probably better off without her. I'm ready." He stepped out of the car and grabbed the box with the puppies, balancing it against his stomach. Brooke told Mercy to stay. She didn't need her companion for this trip.

Together the three of them approached the front door. She saw the conflict in Jonas's eyes even though she thought he might be trying to hide it. He was processing his son's words and might need a minute. She moved slowly, taking in the area.

The home now sported a large play area with a swing set and other items necessary for a child to cut loose and have fun. Brooke raised her hand to knock, but before she connected with the wood, the door swung open. Cassie smiled her greeting. Brooke decided she was probably the only one who noticed the stress in the smile. "Hi, glad you could make it," Cassie said.

Brooke made the introductions. Felix ducked his

head and studied the puppies until Jonas nudged him. He glanced up. "Hi."

"Welcome. Come on in and I'll introduce you to the troops." She led the way through the lobby and into a large area that had been converted into a den. Several children sat at a picnic table playing checkers. Four others who looked between the ages of eight and fourteen stood on a mat in front of the large-screen television and jumped up and down as a cart raced over a rail track. "That's good exercise," Brooke said.

"Fun, too," Jonas agreed. He rubbed his right shoulder and Brooke frowned.

"Are you all right?"

"Caught my sore shoulder against the door during your fancy driving." He shook his head. "I'm fine."

The puppies scrambled to get a foothold on the side of the box only to slide back to the bottom. Cassie peered over the edge and hooked one under his chubby belly. "Children, look who's come to visit."

Felix set the box on a side table and picked up the other pup.

The children gathered, their oohs and ahhs filling the room. Brooke scanned the room looking for the little boy she'd seen a couple of months ago. Her gaze landed on a brown-haired boy about seven years old. He stood back from the group, his face pale, eyes haunted. He blinked and started to leave. Brooke made her way to Felix and whispered in his ear. "There by the door."

Felix nodded and slipped through the children. Brooke wandered behind him. Jonas helped with the other puppy and children, but she could feel his gaze on her back. Felix held out the puppy to little Tommy. "Wanna hold him?"

Tommy's eyes went wide. "Me?"

"Sure. You looked like you wanted to."

"Why don't you sit on the couch?" Brooke asked. "Then you can hold him in your lap."

Tommy scooted to the sofa and climbed up. His little legs stuck off the end, the laces of one tennis shoe dangling toward the floor. He held up his hands. Through the side window, Brooke noted that Cassie and Jonas had managed to lure the other children outside. They all sat in a circle, legs spread to allow the puppy to run from one child to the other. Laughter floated through the screen door in the kitchen.

Brooke parked herself on the edge of the other couch and let Felix and Tommy talk. Felix chatted, keeping up a running monologue about all kinds of different things. The one Tommy seemed to respond to the most was football. The minutes passed. She didn't want to rush them, but when the puppy fell asleep in Tommy's lap, she nodded to Felix. Felix cleared his throat. "Hey, Tommy, I hear you're having some trouble sleeping at night."

Tommy froze. Brooke flipped through a magazine and pretended not to pay attention.

"Yeah." Tommy's soft whisper reached her ears.

"When my mom left, I couldn't sleep at night either."

"She left?"

"Uh-huh. She left when I was about three so I don't remember much about her but I keep thinking she's coming back." He glanced away. "I don't think she is, though."

"I'm sorry," Tommy said.

"Me, too." Silence hung between the two boys. She wanted to jump in, but held herself still. She could see Tommy struggling with something, trying to make up his mind about whether or not he wanted to let the words out.

"My mom and dad died in a car wreck and I didn't have anyone else who wanted me to come live with them."

"That's tough."

Brooke thought her heart might simply shatter at the pain being shared by the two boys. She blinked away the tears and drew in a steadying breath. She had to keep it together.

Felix scratched the puppy's head and he wiggled awake, yawning. "Is that why you're having trouble sleeping?"

Tommy swallowed and lifted the puppy to his face. He spoke to the animal. "No, it's cuz of my dreams. I see him in my dreams."

"See who?" Felix asked. He scratched the puppy's back.

Brooke trembled. Finally. Felix met her gaze, his eyes wide. Brooke gave him a thumbs-up and he straightened his shoulders a bit before leaning closer and settling a hand on Tommy's shoulder. "You can tell me, Tommy. Who do you see?"

Tommy drew in a deep breath. "What's the puppy's name?"

Felix wilted a fraction, but Brooke gave him an encouraging nod.

"He doesn't have one," Felix said. "You want to name him?"

"I'd name him Buster if he was mine," Tommy said.

"His name is Buster then."

Tommy finally looked at Felix. "In my dreams, I see the man with the white hair. He's big and scary and I don't like him. He had a gun and I'm afraid he's going to come get me and shoot me."

White hair? She couldn't take it anymore. "It's okay,

Tommy, you don't have to be afraid of him," Brooke soothed as she moved over to sit beside the boy. The puppy stretched to lick Tommy's nose then scrunched back down to nibble on his fingers.

Tommy gave a low giggle that faded as fast as it appeared. He looked up at Brooke. "I don't?"

"No way." She pulled out her badge. "See this?"

"Yes."

"You know what it means?"

"It means you're a police officer?"

"That's right. Do you remember we talked once before?"

"Uh-huh."

"We're here and we're going to protect you so you don't have to be afraid. Can you tell me a little more about the man with the white hair?"

Tommy clamped his lips together and shook his head.

"Okay then, if I get someone to come, could you help that person draw a picture of the man you saw?"

Tommy shrugged. "Maybe. I mostly saw his back. In my dream, I mean."

"Right. In your dreams." Brooke pulled up a picture of Congressman Jeffries on her phone and showed it to the child. "Was this the man with the white hair?"

He studied the picture, his forehead creased. Then lifted his shoulder again. "I don't know." He looked away and swallowed hard.

Brooke slipped to her knees to look the little boy straight in the eye. She cupped his cheeks. "I want you to know that I'm very proud of you for telling Felix about the man with the white hair. You can go to sleep without worrying about him. He can't hurt you, okay? Even if you see him in your dreams, you can tell yourself that he can't hurt you." Tears filled his eyes, and he blinked until they ran down his cheeks. Brooke swiped them away and he leaned into her arms, the puppy squirming between them. "Okay?" she pressed.

He nodded against her shoulder. "Okay."

Brooke reached over and grasped Felix's fingers and squeezed. He returned the pressure and she looked up to see a glint of pride in his eyes.

She turned to find Jonas staring at them and thought she saw a hint of moisture in his eyes before he blinked and leaned down to pick up one of the children that had attached herself to his leg. Brooke hadn't heard them come in from outside.

The little girl was about four years old. She patted his cheek and stuck her thumb in her mouth. Jonas held her like a pro. Like a natural father. A wave of pain swept through Brooke so strong and so great it nearly knocked her to her knees.

He was a good father to Felix and deserved to have more children. As many as he wanted. And she could never be the one to give him that. She really needed to remember that.

Brooke straightened and cleared her throat. "All right, Tommy, thank you very much."

"Can I play with the puppy now?"

"Sure. Most of the other children are outside with his brother. You want to take him to join the fun?"

Tommy nodded and she helped him off the couch, the canine clutched in his little arms.

"You did great, Felix," Jonas murmured to his son. Felix let a smile slip across his lips before he managed to get it under control. He gave a careless shrug, not fooling anyone in the room with his nonchalant attitude. "I'd better go make sure they don't hurt the puppies." He sauntered out the door, but Brooke thought his back seemed straighter, his head held higher.

"Wow," Jonas breathed. "Was that my kid?"

"Yeah, he did great. Now I need to call Gavin and fill him in and get a sketch artist out here to work with Tommy." Nicholas stepped through the door. Brooke lifted a brow. "Everything all right?"

"I'm just here to make sure you get home safe."

"Great. I was just getting ready to call Gavin." She motioned him to follow her into one of the back rooms. "I don't want the others hearing this, but I want to put it on speaker so you can listen in."

The phone rang twice before Gavin picked up. "Gavin here."

The snap in his voice made Brooke pause for only a second. "Hi, Gavin. I've got an interesting development. Tommy said that the man he saw in his dreams not only had a gun, but white hair."

"Okay."

She drew in a breath. "The congressman has white hair."

Nicholas frowned at her boldness, but she just waited.

The silence from Gavin made her shift, her nerves tightening as she wondered if she'd gone too far. Then Gavin cleared his throat. "Right. He has gray hair, not white. And don't forget, he was shot, too. And it wasn't self-inflicted."

"I know, Gavin, I just..."

"So let's keep our focus where it needs to be."

"What if the congressman's son shot him?" Nicholas asked.

"What?"

"What if Michael was trying to defend himself against his father? What if the senator shot Michael, but Michael managed to get a shot off, too?"

Gavin went silent again and Brooke wondered if he was going to hang up. "Where's the gun, Nicholas? The weapon was never recovered, remember? Harland was lying in a pool of blood, practically unconscious when help arrived. The crime scene unit searched the scene. Law enforcement searched the scene. Your very own team members searched the scene. Are you suggesting that all of those professionals missed finding the weapon?"

Nicholas sighed. "Of course not, but—"

"And what about the car that was seen speeding away?"

Nicholas shook his head and Brooke could tell he wished he'd kept his mouth shut.

"It still could have been Erin Eagleton," she said. "Her necklace—with a charm with her initials—was found there and she's disappeared. She was Michael Jeffries's girlfriend. She's still a viable suspect."

"Yes, she is," Gavin agreed. "And there may be others we haven't discovered yet." He paused. "Look, I'm not as close-minded as I'm coming across. If Harland is involved in something, I want to know it. I just have a hard time believing it and don't want to miss finding the real killer because we're distracted and focused on the wrong trail."

Or we miss Harland being the killer because we're distracted and focused on the wrong trail, she thought. But decided against pointing it out. Nicholas met her gaze and she knew he was thinking the exact same thing.

* * *

Jonas watched out the window as the children and their guardians romped with the puppies. They looked happy and well-adjusted. Someone looking in from the outside wouldn't know the turmoil these kids had already experienced in their young lives.

When Brooke had hugged little Tommy and let him rest his head against her, a fierce longing had gripped Jonas. He wanted Brooke. Not just as a casual friend, but as a lifelong partner, someone to walk through the ups and downs of life with him. Someone to share more children with. Jonas headed down the hall to the room where she and Nicholas had taken their conversation.

Her low voice drew him to the door. "Yes, he's sure. White hair." She listened then shrugged. "I know the congressman has gray hair, and not white, but combine the other factors of a moon and it being at night, maybe his gray hair looked white to Tommy. I'm not trying to put words in his mouth, but maybe he's just not using the word *gray*, but that's what he means." She paused and her gaze met his even as she listened. He started to leave, not wanting to butt in where he shouldn't, but she held up a hand to stall his departure. "I get that, Gavin, but it's still possible Tommy is describing Jeffries. Could you set it up with Cassie to have a sketch artist work with him?" More silence, more pacing. "All right. Any word on Erin Eagleton? I still think she may be the key to solving this thing." A heavy sigh slipped from her. "Okay. Thanks." She hung up and turned to Jonas. "Well, we'll see what happens."

"Is he going to send a sketch artist?" Jonas asked.

She nodded. "As soon as he can set it up."

"You really think you'll get an accurate picture of the man Tommy saw that night?"

"I don't know, but I think it's worth a try."

The clamor of laughter and children's high-pitched voices reached them. "They're coming back in," Jonas said.

Felix held the two puppies. "It looks like it's going to rain."

Brooke nodded. "It's time for us to leave." Tommy raced forward and wrapped his arms around her waist. Brooke seemed startled for a split second before she dropped to her knees to hug him. "I'll come back soon, all right?"

Tommy nodded and Jonas thought Brooke might break down and cry. He took a step forward, but she blinked a few times then smiled at Cassie. "Thanks for letting us come."

"Of course. Anytime. Stay safe."

Tommy went to Cassie and she picked him up and planted a kiss on his cheek. Tommy smiled and leaned his head against her shoulder.

Brooke led the way out.

Felix climbed into the back of the vehicle, the box clutched closely to him, the playful puppies worn out and sound asleep. Brooke let Mercy out to take care of business. In short order, she was back at the vehicle. She jumped into her special spot and lay down, her head between her paws.

Jonas glanced at the clock. He'd been gone from the clinic a good while. "I'm going to check in with Claire."

"Sure. Just put your blindfold back on. I'll let you know when you can take it off." She glanced into the backseat at Felix, who rolled his eyes, but complied with a small smile. She didn't think he was terribly annoyed. Her phone buzzed and she glanced at the text. "Nicholas and Chase are going to escort us back to your office. They're working in conjunction with the local police to set up a 24/7 guard."

He nodded. "All right. I'm not going to fight the idea. Felix might not like, it, but I'll do whatever I've got to do to keep him safe."

A groan came from the backseat. They ignored him. "And yourself," she said.

"Right." Jonas dialed his office's number and got Claire on the second ring as Brooke aimed the vehicle down the long drive.

"All is fine here," Claire assured him. "Slow, but fine. We had a couple of people who wanted to come in, but I explained you had an emergency."

He sighed. "I'm going to have to find someone to help out."

"Do you want me to put a call out for resumes?"

"Yes. And then start checking references. I need someone fast."

"What about Graham Brown? He called last week asking about an interview."

Jonas pictured the son of his father's best friend. "Is he back in town?"

"He is." Claire went on to list a few other possibilities and Jonas listened with half an ear. His mind kept circling back to the side mirror and wondering who could be behind the attacks on them. "Jonas?"

"Right. Sorry. I'm here. Just…call whoever you think best and set up interviews with me. I'll take it from there."

"All right, I can do that."

Jonas hung up, and peeked through the bottom edge

of his blindfold to see the screen and dialed his home to check his voice mails. Three hang-ups. One from his mother who lived in Richmond, Virginia. Two from his sister who wanted to know what happened to his house.

He deleted those and went to the next message.

"Give me the phone or your kid is dead."

Click.

ELEVEN

Brooke heard Jonas's indrawn breath and looked over to see the part of his face beneath the blindfold drain of color. "What is it?"

He shook his head and hung up the phone. "Nothing. Not here," he said in almost a whisper. She glanced in the backseat. Felix had his head against the window, the blindfold covering his eyes. He gave all appearances of being asleep, but that didn't mean he was. She nodded. Whatever Jonas had heard on the phone he didn't want to repeat in front of Felix.

Nicholas and Chase had fallen in with her about ten minutes ago as she'd pulled onto the highway. One in front and one behind.

"Are the police going to be waiting when we get to the office?" Jonas asked, his voice low.

"Yes."

He nodded and she saw his Adam's apple bob. "Good."

"You checked your messages?"

"I did."

She looked in the rearview mirror. She thought maybe Felix really was asleep. "Felix?" He didn't move. "You can take off your blindfold now." Still no response. "You can take yours off, too, Jonas." He did. She glanced at his phone. "Do I need to take a listen?"

"Yes."

"Pull it up for me and hand me your Bluetooth." She put the device against her ear and Jonas played the message. "Give me the phone or your kid is dead."

She blinked. "Is that the only one?"

"Yes. There were some hang-ups before that."

"We'll see if we can trace the number," she said. She handed him her phone and his Bluetooth device, replacing it with hers. "Dial number 1 on speed dial." He followed her instructions, then handed the phone back to her. "Gavin. I need you to get a subpoena for the Parker residence phone records." In a low voice, with frequent glances at Felix in the backseat, she explained the threatening phone call.

"I'll get Fiona on it. What else?" Fiona Fargo, a whiz with any kind of technology, would have what they needed within a few hours. If that long.

"That's it for now." She started to hang up. "No wait, Gavin?"

"Yes?"

"I think we need to wear our Kevlar vests 24/7, Jonas and Felix included." She ignored Jonas's sharp look.

"It's come to that, has it?"

"I just want to be prepared."

"I'll have some waiting for you when you get to the office. We'll pass them in and they can put them on before they get out of the vehicle."

Sounded like a good plan to her. "Our ETA is about five minutes."

"Slow down and take your time. It'll be a little longer than that before I can deliver the vests."

"Got it." She lifted her foot from the gas. "See you soon." She hung up and told Jonas the plan.

"Vests?" he asked quietly.

"I think it's a needed precaution."

A sigh slipped from him and she couldn't help reaching out and patting his hand. "I'm sorry, I know it's an imposition."

He grasped her fingers before she could pull them back. "Yes, it is, but we'll manage. I just want Felix safe. That's the most important thing."

"You're a good dad, Jonas."

He tilted his head then turned to look in the backseat. "He's really in a deep sleep."

"Yes. He zonked out a few minutes after we left the children's home."

"I don't think he's been sleeping well. I hear him get up at night sometimes. If I ask him if he's all right, he says he's fine and gets back in bed, but I don't know. I don't know what to do for him."

"It's a tough time right now."

"Very." He paused. Then, "As for me being a good dad, I'm not so sure about that."

"I am."

He fell silent as he studied her. She resisted squirming and concentrated on driving.

Ten minutes later, Brooke followed Nicholas as he turned into the parking lot of the veterinary office. Chase swung in behind her. In the rearview mirror, she noticed Felix rubbing his eyes and looking around. Two squad cars took up two spaces. Jonas tensed and rubbed a hand down his face. "I guess this is where it all begins?"

She nodded. "You'll have full coverage from this point on."

"Oh man," Felix said. "Say hello to Big Brother."

"Stop," Jonas said mildly.

Another car pulled in beside them. Brooke tensed as the officers threw open their doors and walked toward the new vehicle. An arm extended out the window. The hand attached to the arm held a badge. Brooke relaxed a fraction. The badge disappeared back into the vehicle and two vests appeared. One of the officers took the vests and brought them over to Brooke. She passed them to Jonas and Felix. "Put these on."

"Seriously?" Felix uttered a disgusted sigh, but complied. "This is getting totally out of control, you know."

"Yeah," Brooke said. "I agree." She looked at the officer. "Any sign of unwanted visitors?"

"No. We've been canvassing the area and the property, doing perimeter searches and everything. It's been quiet."

"Well, we're here now so that's liable to change."

He lifted a brow. "Yes, ma'am. And we're ready."

Jonas and Felix had the vests on. Felix settled the puppies in his lap. He tapped the vest. "These are really going to help with that head shot. I'm impressed."

Jonas shot his son a frown. Brooke would have laughed if the situation hadn't been so serious. She caught Felix's eye in the rearview mirror and realized he was using sarcasm to deal with the stress. "You'd make a great cop, Felix. You're a natural."

He rolled his eyes, but not before she caught a flash of surprised pleasure.

With the other officers surrounding them, the vests not as much protection as she would have liked, they escorted Jonas and Felix into the building. Claire's eyes went wide and her mouth formed a silent O. Jonas gave her a sheepish look. "Hi, Claire."

"What is going on?"

"It's a long story."

"Obviously."

Brooke stepped forward. "Have you had any trouble while Jonas has been gone?"

"No, not a bit." She paused. "Then again, what do you mean by trouble?"

"Anything out of the ordinary? People coming in who shouldn't be here?" She glanced at Jonas then back to Claire. "People calling and leaving messages that make you uneasy?"

Claire frowned and shook her head. "No, nothing like that." Another pause. "Except maybe the guy who came in right after lunch."

"What about him?"

"He said he was an old friend of Jonas's and wanted to talk to him."

"What was weird about that?"

"When I told him Jonas wasn't here, but he could leave his name and number, he waved me off and said he'd find him later."

Brooke leaned in. "Can you describe him for me?"

She shrugged. "Around six feet tall, dark hair, dark eyes. Nothing that really stood out to me. Just an average-looking nice guy." She snapped her fingers. "Oh, and he had on one of those muscle shirts. He had a tattoo on his right shoulder."

"A muscle shirt in March?"

"The cold didn't seem to bother him."

"Do you have security cameras in here?" she asked.

"Yes."

"Let's look at the footage."

Ten minutes later, Jonas worked the mouse and brought up the video of a man entering the front door.

He walked up to the desk and Claire greeted him. They talked for less than a minute, then he turned and left. She looked at Jonas. "Do you recognize him?"

"No."

"I do," Felix said. She turned to find him staring at the monitor. He looked up and caught her gaze. "That's the guy that was out at the cliffs the day I found the phone."

Jonas shook his head. "This is getting beyond crazy."

Brooke nodded. "I won't argue that statement. Can you zoom in a little more on him?"

Jonas did and she stepped back. "Nicholas, take a look. Do you recognize him?"

"No. You?"

"No."

Nicholas and Chase both moved closer. Nicholas narrowed his eyes. "So the guy on the cliffs and the guy who came in here are one and the same," he said.

Jonas turned to look at Claire. "You didn't recognize him from anywhere? Ever seen him before?"

She paled. "No."

"Did he see the flyers on the desk?"

Her eyes shot to the stack of flyers still stacked. "I don't think so." She swallowed and gave a nervous groan. "I got so busy answering the phones, I never put the posters up."

"It's all right," Brooke soothed. "It's probably a good thing. If he'd seen the poster in the window and recognized the man in the picture, he might not have been so cordial." She pursed her lips and looked at Nicholas and Chase. "I think we need to really up the security around here."

"Or move them to a safe house," Nicholas said.

"No," Felix said. "I don't want to move to some safe

house. I've got school." Felix flashed them all a hard look and turned to head to the back of the office. Probably to their temporary room to sulk.

Jonas pressed his fingers against his eyes. Moving to a safe house would severely hamper his business—although being dead wouldn't do it much good either. And Felix's safety came first, of course.

He sighed. He didn't have a partner. He'd have to close down and that would put Claire out of work for however long it took to solve this. "Is there any way you can just keep us safe here? I think Felix would be all right at school, especially if he stays on campus and doesn't go anywhere alone." He shot his son a questioning look. Felix nodded, his expression earnest.

Brooke and her two coworkers exchanged glances. "It's possible," she said. "It would just be easier at a safe house."

"I understand that, but..."

"But?" Brooke asked.

"Ah! I don't know." Jonas ran a hand through his hair. If he made the wrong decision his son could be killed. "Give me a bit to think about it."

Brooke nodded. "Fine, just don't take too long."

Jonas paced, his thoughts swirling. He wanted to do the right thing by Felix. Had to do the right thing. As hard as it might be. Ten minutes was all it took to figure out what he needed to do. While he thought and paced, Brooke and Nicholas discussed the case and outlined several alternatives that might work to keep him and his son safe. For now...

Fine. A safe house. Or... He looked at Brooke. "Excuse me. I'm going to talk to Felix. I'll be right back." He walked to the back and found Felix sitting on the cot, eyes glued on the screen in front of him. "Felix?"

His son didn't hear him. Or was ignoring him. Jonas gave him the benefit of the doubt and walked over to tap the kid's tennis shoe. Felix pulled the earbuds down. "What?"

"Sir?"

"Sir?" Felix dutifully repeated with a miniature roll of his eyes. Jonas thought about snatching the Kindle from his hands and demanding an apology. But that would only add fuel to the fire. He controlled his impulse. He didn't have time to get into a power struggle with his son. "We need to make a decision and I want your input."

"I already gave my input. I'm not going to a safe house."

"Even if it means keeping you alive? Keeping me alive?"

That seemed to catch his attention. "Are you in danger because of me?"

"No. No, I…well, I don't know. It doesn't matter the reason behind the danger as far as this decision is concerned. What matters is keeping us safe." He sighed. "Will you think about it for a few minutes? And I mean put aside what you want and think about the danger, about being willing to do whatever it takes to stay safe."

Felix shook his head. "I'm not going to some dumb safe house. I'll run away."

Jonas wanted to hit something. Sometimes Felix's stubborn streak was enough to send him over the edge. "Think about it, Felix." Jonas got up to give his son some space. Give himself some space.

He returned to the front office to find Brooke and Nicholas still talking. When he stepped into the area, she lifted a brow at him. He shrugged and pinched the bridge of his nose. An idea formed. "What if I sent Felix to live with my parents for a while? What if we just removed him from the equation?"

"No way!" Felix said from behind him. Jonas spun to see that his son had come into the room. Now Felix moved backward, toward the door again. "I'm not doing that."

"Felix, your life is at stake here!" Jonas couldn't help the shout. He drew in another deep breath and closed his eyes, praying for some control. "You don't want to go to a safe house, I get that. This might be the best alternative. And it would get you out of the area."

"But—"

"I don't like it either, but we may not have a choice."

Felix glared. "You just want to get rid of me. Abandon me the same way Mom did."

The words stabbed dagger sized holes in his heart. His son knew exactly how to push the buttons that hurt the most. He stared at Felix, refused to let his son look away. "You know that's not true."

"All I know is that you want to send me away. I'm not going." He pushed open the door that led to the back, where the exam rooms and their temporary living quarters were. "Something good finally happened today and I felt—" He continued his backward walk and shook his head. "No. I'm not going. Why can't we just go home? I want to go home."

"We can't—"

"I know that." Felix's fingers curled into tight fists. "I know." He disappeared and Jonas bit his tongue on the words he wanted to fling at his son's back. Not words of anger, words of love, promises to never abandon him. But now wasn't the time. Not with the silent onlookers.

He sighed. "I'll talk to him again." As soon as his blood pressure settled down. "If we go into a safe house, how long would we be there?"

"Unfortunately, there's no way to tell."

Jonas nodded. He shoved out of the vest and set it on one of the waiting room chairs. "Claire, why don't you go on home? I'll take care of the rest of the day."

His assistant glanced at the clock. "Not much day left anyway. I'll see you tomorrow?"

He hesitated. "Call before you come, all right?"

She frowned then shrugged. "Sure." She left with a wave.

Nicholas and Chase pulled Brooke to the side and another intense conversation ensued. Jonas figured Felix had had enough time to cool off and went to find him. His heart ached at his son's pain and he had to fix it. Not that he really believed he could actually "fix" it, but he had to try and do *something.* Convince him that going to a safe house wasn't an act of punishment, but an act of love. Brooke had told him he was a good dad. Now he needed to put those words into action and stand firm in his decision.

He glanced in at the two cots that formed an L-shape. His under the window, Felix's on the adjoining wall. No Felix. With a frown, he looked to the bathroom. The door was cracked. "Felix?" He crossed the room and peeked in the bathroom. "Hey, where are you?"

When he didn't get an answer, he opened the door to expose the whole bath area. Shower to the right, sink straight ahead, toilet and linen closet area to the left.

But no sign of his son.

Panic started to creep in, but before letting it grow further, Jonas wanted to check the rest of the building. He started with the exam rooms, then his office, the storage area and out through the swinging door connected to the kennel. Nothing.

He froze, his brain spinning. He turned to the door that led out to the back and found it unlocked.

He never left it unlocked.

A wave of nausea swept over him.

Felix was gone.

TWELVE

"Felix is gone," Jonas said from behind her. Brooke spun to find him standing in the doorway that led from the back.

"What?"

"He's gone." He rubbed a hand over his face, his weariness palpable.

"There's no way anyone could have taken him," Brooke said.

Jonas shook his head. "I don't think anyone took him. I think he left on his own. I'm pretty sure he slipped out the back door."

"That door doesn't sound the alarm when opened?"

"Not if the alarm is cut off. Felix knows the code."

She looked at Chase, who bolted for the door. Nicholas spoke rapidly on the phone, then hung up and followed after Chase.

"We'll search around here, you start calling friends," Chase said. He shut the door behind him.

Brooke snapped her gaze to Mercy who lay near a line of waiting room chairs. "She's not a search and rescue dog, but she's had some training. I'll see if she can pick up his scent."

"Felix slept on the cot in the back last night, the one on the left as you walk in the room."

"Good. Mercy, heel." The dog leapt to her feet and rushed over to plant herself at Brooke's side. Brooke led the way to the back with Jonas and Mercy at her side. In the room, she stopped at the cot, snagged the pillow and held it to Mercy's nose. "Find him, girl." The dog sniffed, nudged it and sniffed again. Then her nose went to the floor, back into the air. She darted out of the bedroom, down the hall and to the back door.

Brooke pushed it open. Mercy darted out. Her nose quivering, she led them to the edge of the property that backed up to another building. Here she stopped, whined, sniffed the ground, tested the air then sat. "She lost the scent."

"What does that mean?"

"Felix could have gotten into a car. Do any of his friends drive?"

"None that I know of. He's thirteen. If he's got older friends, they'd be from school and I don't know about them." He paused. "Actually, some of the guys on the track team drive, but he doesn't hang out with them."

"That you know of."

"Yes." He paced three steps then back. "What if he was picked up by the people after him? What if they were watching, just waiting for a chance to grab him?"

Brooke hated that he voiced her thoughts. She'd been hoping he wouldn't think about that. "Let's just pray he contacts you soon or that we find him." She looked around. "Your security cameras won't reach this far, will they?"

"No."

Brooke led Mercy back to the office and let her inside.

"We need to find him," Brooke said to Jonas. "Would you call the friend he was with the night someone broke in?"

"Of course." He reached for his phone, his face pale, jaw tight. She figured he might be experiencing a wide range of emotions. Anger for Felix for leaving, fear his decision would result in tragic consequences. Indecision about what to do next.

Brooke frowned and set out a bowl of water for Mercy. The dog lapped it up.

While Jonas spoke on his phone, Brooke called the local PD and requested a BOLO be issued. It was a long shot, but sometimes they got good response from a Be On the Lookout order. She snapped a picture of the framed photo on Jonas's desk. Felix stared at the camera, a half smile on his lips as if he had secrets to share, but wasn't interested in doing so. She sent that to Fiona. "Get this to all the officers and tell them to be on the lookout for him, will you?"

"Consider it done." Fiona disconnected without bothering to say goodbye.

Jonas hung up and shook his head. "They haven't seen him."

"Can you think of where else he would he go?"

"No. I don't know." He started his pacing again, from one end of the office to the other. "I can't think. Travis is the only friend he really hangs out with. They're on the track team together and while he and the rest of his teammates get along, they don't do much together. He has some acquaintances from the youth group, but he's not close enough to any of them to go to one of their houses. At least I don't think so." Guilt flashed across his features and he came to a stop in front of her. "And that's my fault. The lack of friends at church."

"Don't go much?"

"No. Not much."

"We need to call them anyway, just to be sure." He nodded. She remembered his strong faith back when they worked together at the kennel and the fact that he always said the blessing before meals. His faith wasn't totally gone. "What happened?"

He gave her a sad smile and a shrug. "Life." He clasped his hands between his knees and looked down. "I think I need to reassess that, though. Make God a priority in my life again." He looked up. "And not just because trouble has found its way into my house. I've actually been thinking about it for a while, feeling…convicted might be the right word."

"I understand that." And she did. She struggled every day with questions for God. Some she asked, some she ignored. Some were just too painful. But she refused to shove Him aside, instead choosing to believe His promises that He had a plan for her future. If she didn't believe that, she wouldn't be able to function on a daily basis. But that didn't mean she couldn't understand what Jonas was saying. Feeling.

"Only now I may have waited too long and Felix is going to suffer the consequences," he said.

"I don't think God works that way. Felix isn't in trouble because you put God on the back burner. He's in trouble because of his choices—and the choices of those after him."

Jonas looked thoughtful and worried all at the same time. "Yes, I know you're right. It's hard not to let those thoughts intrude, though."

Jonas stayed quiet, then pulled his phone from his pocket. "I'll call the school and ask the principal to get a list of any older kids that Felix has been seen hanging around with."

Before he could punch in the number, Nicholas opened the front door and stepped inside. Jonas hesitated, waiting, his eyes hopeful. "Anything?"

"Nothing."

Chase brought up the rear and shut the door behind him. "We took the car and searched up and down the road. No sign of him, I'm sorry."

Jonas slumped against the wall and stared at his feet.

"Hey, do you need to sit down?" Brooke asked.

He lifted his head, his eyes weary, face drawn. "No. I need to find my son."

"We'll find him, Jonas." She stepped forward and rested a hand on his arm. "Chase, could you call the school and get any information about students Felix may have hung around with who have cars?"

"Of course." Chase stepped outside to make the call.

"We've got to have more coverage on this place," she said to Nicholas while Jonas held the phone to his ear and paced the floor. He went to the window every other pace and looked out only to resume his going-nowhere journey of back and forth.

"You know as well as I do it's a manpower issue, not a willingness issue," Nicholas said.

"I know that, but we're talking about people's lives. If this is related to Michael Jeffries and Rosa Gomez's deaths and the congressman's shooting, then we know they won't hesitate to do whatever it takes to get rid of them. The thug who is after them has already set fire to a children's home, Nicholas. He's desperate." She paused. "Or just has no conscience. Or both."

"I know that," Nicholas said, "but we're going to have

to get Gavin's, maybe even Margaret's, clearance on it." He ran a hand through his blond hair. "That phone call I got before we went to look for Felix was from Harland Jeffries. He's ready to talk to us first thing in the morning."

She noticed Jonas had hung up and was listening in. "I'll have to go, Jonas," she said.

"Of course you will. You can't babysit me 24/7."

"I don't consider it babysitting," she said and frowned. She didn't want him to think she felt obligated. "I care about you. I want to make sure you're safe." His eyes warmed and he cleared his throat but didn't look away from her. She was the first to drop her gaze as heat started to rise from the base of her neck. She could almost see Nicholas's amusement at her discomfort. That was fine. He could be entertained as long as he kept his mouth shut. "There will be cops all over this place, watching out for you and looking for Felix."

He nodded then straightened as his eyes sharpened. "Wait a minute. Felix said he wanted to go home."

"What?"

"Right before he walked out. He said he wanted to go home. What if he did?"

Brooke frowned and shot a look at Nicholas. "It's possible. You only live about a mile from here, right?"

Nicholas nodded. "Absolutely. Let's go."

They made their way to the cars and headed to Jonas's house. Less than two minutes later, they pulled to the curb and climbed from the vehicles. Brooke placed a hand on Jonas's arm to keep him from bolting to the house. "Give me the keys and stay in the car, will you?"

"You think someone else might be in there besides Felix?"

"I don't want to take a chance."

He fished the keys from his pocket and handed them over to her. "I don't like this," he muttered. "I don't like it at all. You could get hurt. I should—"

"I have the training and the gun. It's better this way."

He almost smiled through the tension and worry over his son—not to mention the fact that it appeared someone wanted him dead. "Right. But I'm staying behind you."

She started to protest, saw the look on his face, the set of his jaw, and stopped. "Stay behind, close but not too close."

He nodded. She walked up the front steps and handed the keys to Nicholas. She could hear the huge fans blowing on the inside. The restoration company had come and gone. She and Nicholas positioned themselves on either side of the door and had their weapons drawn. She could feel Jonas behind her. Still, tense, desperate to find Felix safe. Adrenaline pounded through her. *Please let him be here, God.*

Nicholas unlocked the front door and twisted the knob. The door swung in. Brooke stepped over the threshold, weapon ready. The smell of smoke still hung in the air, but it wasn't overpowering. At least she could breathe. The foyer was clear. Nicholas stepped around her and headed up the stairs. Concerned, she watched him, knowing the roar of the fans would mask any sound an intruder might make. Then again, they would hide their arrival, too.

She looked to the left. To the right. Nothing so far. Jonas slipped inside and moved to stand with his back to the wall.

She waited for Nicholas's call as she moved into the kitchen. Neat, orderly, nothing disturbed. She backed out and moved into the den, noticing Jonas still in the same place, hands clenched, a muscle in his jaw jumping.

In the den, the smell was stronger. Cleaning solution and old smoke. She ran a hand over the couch. Still slightly damp.

"Clear!"

"Clear!" Brooke echoed. "Did you find any evidence of Felix?" She shouted to be heard.

"No." He came down the stairs. Brooke slid her weapon into her holster. "You?" he asked.

"No," she sighed, worry ramping her pulse back up. "He's not here."

"Nothing?" Jonas asked.

She turned to face him as he stepped into the den. "No. Sorry."

He blew out a sigh and shook his head. "Okay, I'm staying here tonight."

She frowned. "I don't know if that's such a great idea."

"Felix wanted to come home. He may wait until nighttime to do that. I'm going to be here in case he does."

She narrowed her eyes. "Fine, but you're not staying here alone."

Nicholas rubbed a hand over his chin. "I've got him covered. I'll take the night shift."

"Good," Brooke said. "Because I think we may be dealing with more than one person. We've got Tommy's white-haired man with the gun and the person who broke into Jonas's house."

"I agree. It's definitely more than one person."

"And unfortunately, I don't think the people causing all of this trouble bother to sleep."

THIRTEEN

Brooke was ready to go by seven the next morning. Harland Jeffries had called to cancel, citing an emergency meeting. She wasn't happy with the man, but decided that worked with their schedule a little better. They planned to track down the missing aide. She'd checked in with Nicholas after a restless night's sleep, worrying about Felix and Jonas.

"Felix called his dad about three hours ago. He told him he was sorry for all the trouble, but he wasn't going to let his dad send him away and was sorry for causing all the trouble and worry."

Brooke sighed. "He doesn't get it, does he?"

"Nope. But I'm glad he's just a runaway at the moment and not a pawn in this deadly game."

"I'm glad, too. I just hope he either comes home or the good guys find him."

"We had officers looking for him all night and no one reported any sign of him. Overall, it was a quiet night, but I'm not holding my breath that the calm is going to last."

Brooke agreed. She just figured it meant the people after Jonas and Felix were busy plotting their next move. The idea set her nerves on edge.

She climbed into her vehicle and Mercy hopped in the back. Nicholas would leave Max behind with Jonas. She drove to Jonas's house, which was only about fifteen minutes from her own. When she pulled to the front curb, Nicholas was standing on the porch waiting. She rolled down the window. "Ready?"

"Yep. We have an extra passenger, though."

Brooke frowned. "Who?"

"Jonas is going with us."

She lifted a brow and felt a twinge of happiness race up her spine at the thought of just being in his presence for most of the day. "All right. Why?"

He walked out to stand next to her car. "I don't feel comfortable leaving him here." He shook his head. "He didn't get much sleep last night. He's worried sick about his kid."

"I don't blame him. I'm worried, too."

"If he stays here, he's going to think and brood about it. Might even take it upon himself to do something stupid like go looking for him."

"Thereby making himself a target," Brooke murmured.

"Exactly."

She nodded. "Can't hurt for him to come along. And we'll be one of the first to know if something happens with Felix." Good or bad, but she left that part out. She glanced in the back. "There's room."

"It's just an hour or so. Pull up tight to the garage and we'll get him in. He can ride in the front with you. I'll make myself at home in the back with the dogs."

"You sure?"

"Yes. I'm going to grab a nap on the way there. Chase is going to tail us to make sure we're not followed and there aren't any more incidents like yesterday's."

"Sounds like a good plan." Brooke pulled to the garage. Jonas must have been watching. The electric door opened and she pulled all the way in as he had his car parked on the far side. Jonas slipped around to the passenger seat and Max and Nicholas settled themselves into the back with Mercy. "Good morning," she said.

"Morning."

He looked so tired. Her heart went out to him. "I won't ask if you slept."

"I kept thinking the phone would ring. Or Felix would walk in the door." He shook his head. "Or something."

She wanted to hug him, to reassure him. "I'm sorry."

"Thanks."

She glanced in the rearview mirror and caught Nicholas's eyes. "Does he know we're coming?"

"No. Didn't want to give him a chance to run."

Brooke nodded. With each passing mile, she was more and more aware of the presence of the man beside her. Nicholas dozed off about fifteen minutes into the drive and a silence fell between her and Jonas.

She noticed he kept looking at his phone and figured he was hoping for a call or a text either from Felix or *about* Felix. Chase stayed with them all the way, sometimes falling back, but never letting her lose sight of him. Her nerves stayed stretched tight. After everything that had already happened, she expected another attempt and stayed on guard, waiting for it to happen. She knew Nicholas would be awake and ready to act. All she would have to do is call his name. This case had them all learning to snag rest when the opportunity presented itself and to be ready to be alert and in action within the blink of an eye.

"We're almost there," Jonas said.

"Yes. Not too much longer." She glanced at him.

"There are officers on your house. If Felix comes home, someone will be there to protect him."

"I know. I feel a bit guilty that I'm not there myself. Or at the office. Or out looking for Felix. That's really what I should be doing."

Nicholas had called it. "Your safety is our priority. You have to stay safe and be there for Felix when he comes home."

"Right."

Brooke pulled to an intersection with a four-way stop. Nicholas stirred in the backseat. "Guess nothing happened."

"Not yet."

He grimaced at her fatalistic response.

She checked the GPS and turned right, then the next left. The gas station sat tucked at the far end of the parking lot. Two people pumped gas. One car sat in front of the front door. "Kind of slow on this Tuesday morning, isn't it? Hope this guy is working," Brooke said.

"He's working," Nicholas said. "I called and said I had a package to deliver. I asked if someone would be there to sign it. The person said Jake would be."

"I take it Jake is the former aide's new name?"

"Yep. According to Fiona."

"God bless Fiona."

Nicholas smiled.

Jonas nodded to the entrance. "You're right when you say it's pretty slow, but people are here."

"Stay here, all right?" Brooke asked.

"I'll be a good boy." He growled the words, making Brooke wonder at his sincerity. She frowned at him and his face softened. "I will. I won't do anything stupid, I promise. I'll just stare at my phone and pray Felix calls me."

Brooke reached over and tucked his hand into hers for a squeeze. "I know it's hard, Jonas. Just don't give up or stop praying."

"I'm not."

Brooke nodded. Nicholas was already out of the car and waiting. "We'll leave the dogs here and be right back. Hopefully this won't take too long."

Before Brooke shut the car off, Jonas rolled the window down. Brooke cut the engine, slipped out of the driver's seat and shut the door. He checked his phone and sighed at the screen. He knew wishing Felix would call wouldn't make it happen, but he couldn't seem to help himself. He looked up to see a young woman carrying a toddler come through the double glass doors. "Don't bother going in there," she said with a roll of her eyes. "Whoever's supposed to be working must have decided he didn't want to anymore. It's a shame leaving the store open like that. Stuff's going to get stolen if the owner doesn't do something fast."

Brooke flashed her badge. "Do you know the owner?"

"No, I'm just passing through. I paid for my gas at the pump, but wanted to get a couple of drinks. I hollered for someone to let 'em know they had customers, but no one came out." She shook her head and walked to her car.

Brooke frowned, not liking where this was going. She caught Nicholas's eye. "I'll check out the store."

Jonas straightened, his attention on the three people, their words filtering through his mind. Where was Paul Harrison aka Jake?

Nicholas waved to Chase, who'd parked at the edge of the lot near the entrance.

"What's up?" he asked.

Brooke explained. Chase pulled his weapon. He and Nicholas entered the store. Over the next several seconds, two more customers filed out. Brooke talked into her phone. Jonas opened the car door, thought about getting out, then shut the door without moving. He'd promised to be a good boy.

"What's going on?" he called to Brooke.

She walked back over to the car. "They're doing a sweep of the store."

Jonas nodded but frowned. "It seems like trouble is following too close or is one step ahead."

"Yes," she murmured. "It does."

She opened the back door and let the dogs out. "Heel."

They sat at her side, eyes on her face, waiting for the next order.

Jonas waited, too. Nicholas finally appeared, weapon holstered and shaking his head. "I didn't find a body. Found some blood on the wall and the floor." Chase came out after him.

Brooke nodded. "Let the dogs search."

Nicholas nodded and Jonas stepped out of the vehicle. Brooke shot him a frown. He leaned against the door and paused to see what would happen next. Brooke led Mercy to the door of the convenience store. The dog shifted impatiently, quivering with the excitement of the hunt that was about to begin. Brooke opened the door. "Seek."

Mercy shot into the building. Jonas moved closer so he could see.

Nicholas let Max loose and also commanded the dog to seek. Nicholas followed him. Chase held his K-9 back. After a second of sniffing and getting his bearings, Max took off around the side of the building.

Jonas wanted to help, to do something besides just

wait. He slipped around to watch Max, who went straight to the Dumpster at the back of the store.

Brooke kept an eye on Mercy, who was doing her best to find something. In the store's back room, Mercy sniffed the blood spatter on the floor, then the wall. She went to the exit and sat. Brooke opened the door and let the dog out. Mercy bounded into the sunshine, her nose quivering, hind end wagging.

Brooke spotted Nicholas at the Dumpster. Max sat and barked three times. Mercy stayed on her trail, straight to the Dumpster. She sat next to Max and barked.

Brooke's gaze met Nicholas's. "We need to look in there."

"I'm afraid so."

She grimaced. "I'll do it." Jonas came around the corner and Brooke's heart clenched at the lines on his face. "You should have stayed in the car," she told him.

"Maybe." But he didn't move.

Brooke grabbed two wooden crates that had been set next to the Dumpster. She stacked one on top of the other and then climbed up.

"You want me to do that?" Nicholas asked.

"I've got it." She'd been with the team long enough that she no longer felt she had to prove herself by taking on some of the more distasteful aspects, but Brooke had promised herself when she started, she'd never back down from doing whatever it was that needed to be done. She knew Nicholas would do the Dumpster diving if she asked. She also knew he knew she wouldn't ask.

"Be careful," Jonas murmured.

Brooke shoved open the lid of the Dumpster. The smell hit her and she jerked back with a grimace. The crates wobbled and she grabbed the edge of the bin to steady herself. Jonas reached out and gripped the wooden piece, righting it and holding it. Nicholas did the same.

"What is it?" Nicholas asked.

She shot him a dark look. "It stinks. Hand me the gloves, will you please?"

She reached down to snag the gloves Nicholas held up to her. She snapped them on, then turned back to the trash. With one finger, she pushed aside the large piece of cardboard that covered the heap. And stilled. She looked down at the men. "I found Mr. Harrison," she said.

Jonas sucked in a deep breath, but still didn't budge. "What happened to him?" he asked.

"Shot. Once in the chest, which probably explains the spatter on the wall and the floor inside. And, if the evidence beneath him is any indication, once in the head after they dumped him in here." She grimaced and climbed down. "I'm guessing whoever killed him didn't want him found too quickly and this was a handy spot to stash the body."

Nicholas shook his head and pulled out his phone. "Should have cleaned up the blood if they didn't want someone looking for him," he muttered. "I'll get a crime scene unit here."

"How did they know?" Jonas asked. "How did they know you'd come looking for him?"

"I don't know," Brooke said, her heart aching for the loss of the life of the young aide. It was wrong. Needless. If only he'd asked for help, told someone what had him so scared. Instead, he'd run away and now he was dead. "However, what I do know is that it's time to catch a killer before someone else dies."

She saw sheer fear sweep across Jonas's face and knew he was thinking of his son—a thirteen-year-old boy, out there by himself being chased by people who didn't hesitate to kill to get someone out of their way.

And Felix had definitely gotten in their way.

She pulled the gloves off and trashed them. "What now?" Jonas asked.

"Now we wait," Brooke said as she pulled a bottle of hand sanitizer from her pocket and used it liberally.

Thirty minutes later, two black vans pulled into the parking lot. "The crime scene unit's here."

"So is the medical examiner," Nicholas said.

Brooke nodded. "We'll let them take over for now."

"I think it's time to ask the congressman about his missing—and now murdered—aide," Chase said.

Nicholas turned to Jonas. "I think it's time you got back in the car. We're going to be here awhile."

Brooke shook her head. "We need to get this case solved or we're going to wind up with one crime scene after another."

FOURTEEN

Jonas took the bag of groceries from Nicholas. "Thanks." It had been a long day. He was wiped out from the fact that he'd been there when they'd found the aide, compounded by the worry that wanted to eat through his heart about Felix. He should have just crashed into the nearest bed. Instead, he found himself cooking dinner.

Nicholas shrugged out of his coat. "I didn't want you out and about going shopping. This is much safer."

"Anything on Felix?" Nicholas took the bag into the kitchen and set it on the counter. He'd turned the fans off for the moment. He'd turn them back on when he didn't have to carry on a conversation.

"No, he's dropped off the radar." Nicholas frowned.

Brooke stepped into the kitchen and grabbed a head of lettuce and a knife from the block near the sink. "I'd suggest that we put his face on the news and bring the public into it, but I'm afraid that would only alert the people after him." She started chopping the lettuce and Jonas grabbed a bowl for her to put it in. "Let's see if the cops can locate him first."

"I'm hoping he comes home," Jonas muttered.

"Yeah." She stopped her chopping and shot him a

sympathetic look. He shook his head and looked at his phone. Something he'd been doing on a regular basis even though he had the ringer turned up to maximum volume.

Together they worked and soon had a good meal on the table. Nicholas joined them, but left to monitor the perimeter with Max after cleaning his plate. Mercy lay on the kitchen floor, ears flicking, nose twitching.

Jonas took his last swallow of tea and set the glass on the table. "Felix is upset, I get that, but to take off like this when he's in danger..." He shook his head.

"He's definitely upset," Brooke said. She reached across the table and snagged his fingers.

He pulled his chair around next to hers. Close enough to allow their shoulders to touch. "I need a different topic of conversation."

"Okay. What do you want to talk about?"

"Tell me what I did wrong. What made you just decide to quit seeing me?"

She stood, her agitation clear. "It wasn't you, Jonas, it was me. Me!" Mercy rolled to her feet, her eyes on her mistress. Jonas didn't move. Brooke paced from one end of the kitchen to the other. Mercy watched her and whined. Brooke stopped and dropped her head, her chin resting on her chest. She took in a deep breath.

Jonas blinked at her distress. "I'm sorry, Brooke, never mind. It's not important, I guess."

"You're an amazing father. You have a depth of love in your heart for Felix that I can only imagine."

"What does that have to do with anything?"

"Do you want more children?"

"Of course. One day." He paused. "Why?" Then his eyes went wide and before she could answer, blurted, "You don't want kids?"

"I want them, I just can't have them."

He froze at her quiet whisper. "What?" She still didn't look at him. He went to her and placed a finger under her chin to lift her eyes to his. "You can't have children?"

"No." A tear slid down her cheek. "I had a hysterectomy when I was eighteen. I was in the car wreck that killed my parents. I was bleeding, they had to do surgery and..." She shrugged away from him, crossing her arms across her stomach, turning her back to him. "I can't have children."

"So you pushed me away because of that? Why didn't you just tell me?" Anger surged through him and he fought to control it, to keep his tongue from releasing the words trembling on the edge. "Do you know how I agonized over what I could have done to send you running?"

"Jonas—"

"I lay awake at night wondering."

"I didn't—"

"I racked my brain trying to figure out how I'd offended you." He stared at her. "Did you really think so little of me that I would reject you because you couldn't have kids?"

"Why not? That's what Carl did."

He went quiet. Then sighed. "Who?"

"My boyfriend at the time of the accident. He was nineteen. I was eighteen. We were in love, you know, going to get married and have a houseful of kids." She rolled her eyes and shook her head. "I came to in the operating room to find out my parents were dead. My grandparents were devastated, but they assured me they would be there for me and we would all get through this."

"I remember your grandparents and how close you were."

"Are. We still are."

"But?"

"But they didn't know that Carl was coming to visit me. He overheard them talking about my hysterectomy and how they were going to tell me that I would never have a child."

Jonas closed his eyes. "And he told you."

"Yeah." She sniffed and swiped her eyes. "He tried to be gentle about it, of course, said he was sorry about my parents, sorry I'd been hurt, but he couldn't be my boyfriend anymore because who knows where we might end up. He wanted to be with someone who could have kids one day. He kissed my forehead and walked out."

Jonas rubbed his eyes. "I'm so sorry, Brooke. But I wasn't Carl, not then and not now."

"I know," she whispered. "I know, but the hurt was just too deep, the scars too many. The day I walked out of that hospital, I swore off relationships. I loved dogs, I loved the law." She glanced at Mercy, who'd dropped back to the floor. "I loved my job. I couldn't let you distract me. I'm sorry. When I realized how you felt—"

"You ran."

"As hard and as fast as I could go." She sighed. "A few months later, I almost worked up the courage to tell you."

"But?"

"But when I came back to talk to you—"

"What? When? You never came back."

"I didn't approach you. I was talking to your former partner and he told me a little about what you were doing. Like the fact that you were continuing to build your life and your career and raising a young son." She shrugged. "I told myself you didn't need me upsetting your apple cart again. So I left before you got back to the office, threw myself into my job and told myself to forget about you."

"And did you?"

She swallowed hard, but didn't look away. "No."

"He never told me you were there."

She shrugged. "I didn't tell him not to say anything. He probably just forgot."

"Well I didn't forget about you. I loved my wife." He frowned. "At least I thought I did. I did my best to be a good husband to her, a good father to Felix, but..." He sighed. "I don't know what went wrong, to be honest. I worked a lot of hours building the vet business. She got lonely and found someone else. After she left, I told myself no more relationships. No more falling in love." He gave her a crooked smile. "But I couldn't seem to help it. I found myself thinking about you. How I'd let you go without too much of a fight and I regretted it."

Her eyes bounced to his mouth then back up. A flush worked its way into her cheeks. He lowered his head and touched his lips to hers. At her response, he moved to deepen the kiss.

And guilt hit him.

He stood and shoved his chair away. "I'm sorry."

She blinked and looked away. "No. I am."

"I need to focus on Felix. I can't—"

"I understand, Jonas. Stop. It's okay."

He nodded and raked a hand through his hair.

Brooke buried her face in her hands and blew out a sigh. When she looked up, he tried to decipher the expression in her eyes, but couldn't figure it out. Anger? Sadness? Resignation? Regret? She stood. "All right. It's time for me to get out of here. There's an officer on the curb. Nicholas has done several sweeps and it's clear for now."

"I feel like I should be out there looking for him. I don't know if I can handle sitting around and waiting." When he caught himself looking at his watch again, he grimaced.

Brooke walked to the door. "You really don't have a choice, Jonas. I understand your conflict, but what if Felix comes looking for you?"

He nodded. "I know. I'll stay put." For now.

She hesitated, her hand hovering over the knob. She looked as though she might say something, then just gave him a weary smile. "Good night, Jonas."

"'Night."

She slipped out the door, her words now echoing in the stillness. *I can't have children.* He walked to the window and spotted the officer on the curb. Brooke pulled away and disappeared down the street. Jonas felt his heart go with her.

FIFTEEN

Brooke let Mercy into the house after a short run around the block. Her mind spun in an endless loop, replaying the "almost kiss" over and over until she wanted to bury her face in her pillow and scream. Why had he done that? What had he seen in her expression to indicate she wanted him to kiss her?

She nearly laughed out loud at that last silent question. She knew exactly what he'd seen. She might as well have stamped *Kiss Me* written across her forehead.

She groaned and dropped onto the couch. It was going to be a long night. She should have volunteered for Jonas's guard duty. At least that would have given her something to do besides stare at her walls and wish she'd grabbed Jonas and given him the kiss of his lifetime. But she hadn't done that.

And frankly, she was glad she hadn't. Sort of. She understood the guilt that he'd been feeling. His son was out there, angry, upset—and a target. He couldn't be having a romantic moment while that was happening. She got that. Not only that, but she kept pushing him away. Only tonight they'd almost kissed. Well, they had kissed. A light kiss that could have been so much more.

She rubbed her eyes. How confused he must be with her words and actions contradicting each other. She sighed. She wasn't doing it on purpose, she was just as conflicted with herself as he probably was.

Her gaze fell on her grandmother's Bible. It sat in its usual spot in the center of the coffee table. Her grandparents had loved her. Had raised her to love God and to seek His will for her life. But every time the subject of her and marriage and children came up, bitterness accompanied it. Since she didn't want to be bitter, she often just refused to think about it.

But now she had to.

She'd told Jonas why she'd pushed him away almost eight years ago and he'd been angry. Hurt. Betrayed. Had she been wrong to keep that to herself and not explain her actions?

Definitely.

She picked up the Bible and let it fall open. Her grandmother's handwriting jumped out at her. Right before Brooke's grandparents had moved to Florida to retire, her grandmother had placed the Bible in Brooke's hands just before they'd pulled away from the closing at the lawyer's office. "Read it, Brooke. Let God be your comfort."

Be my comfort, God. Show me how to lean on You and not be bitter.

She closed the Bible, stood and walked to the window to glance into the yard. Mercy went to the door and whined. Brooke let her out and stepped onto the back porch steps to watch the animal roam the yard, sniffing, tail wagging. She snagged something from the bushes and trotted to drop the neighbor kid's baseball at her feet. "Thanks, Mercy. I think I've created a monster."

She picked it up and made a note to return it. One day, one was going to go through her window.

Her phone buzzed. She snagged it and found a text from Gavin. This is what Tommy and the sketch artist came up with.

Brooke zoomed in on the computerized composite and gave a disappointed sigh. She texted back. It could be Jeffries or not.

I know. It's inconclusive. I spoke with Tommy myself. He still says he never left the home that night.

Still afraid he'll be in trouble if he says it.

Yes. So right now we have nothing on Jeffries.

She was sure he was relieved over that. Brooke still wasn't convinced Jeffries was innocent. Great. Thanks.

Welcome.

She shoved the phone into her back pocket. "Come on, Mercy, we'd better get some sleep while we can. No telling when the phone will ring again."

Mercy started to trot back toward Brooke, then turned and froze, her attention suddenly focused on the area behind her.

The night air seemed to quiver, then go still. Brooke frowned and rose, rubbing her arms against the chill that was only partially due to the weather. "What is it, girl?"

Mercy glanced back at Brooke then started toward the back of the fence. A low growl escaped her and Brooke's adrenaline kicked into high gear. She reached for her weapon.

The one that wasn't there.

She'd left it on the end table next to the recliner. "Mercy. Come!"

The dog immediately stopped, but kept her focus on whatever had captured her attention. She whined and Brooke knew the dog wanted to obey, but also wanted to go after whatever was near the fence. "Mercy. Come."

Mercy barked, but obeyed. She came to Brooke's side and sat, her entire body tense. Brooke looked toward the bushes and the trees that lined the other side of her fence. For the first time she worried that someone could climb one of the trees and drop into her backyard. "Come on, girl, I'm not liking this. Inside. Now."

Brooke forced the dog through the door, followed her inside and went to retrieve her weapon from the end table. She then spun on her heel and went back out the door, shutting the dog inside. Mercy barked at her, but Brooke wanted to know what was bothering the animal so much. And she wanted to make sure nothing happened to the dog. If someone had a weapon, they'd go for Mercy first, most likely, take her out of the picture. And since Mercy didn't have her vest on, Brooke wouldn't take the chance.

She walked through her backyard to where the waist-high bushes met the back of the fence. "Is anyone there? Hello?" The tree rustled above her and she swung the weapon up. "Come down. Now."

A dark-clad figure slipped from the tree, landed on the other side of the wooden fence and ran.

Mercy's barking reached a frenzied pitch from inside the house.

Brooke raced for the gate, threw open the latch and

headed in the direction she thought her would-be intruder might have gone. Her shoulders itched. She didn't have her vest on but knew if she took the time to get it the guy would be long gone.

She exited onto the street and came to a stop. From the trees in her backyard, the only direction to go was over the neighbor's fence directly opposite hers or through the small area of woods onto the main street.

She figured he'd go for the street.

Only she didn't see him anywhere. The faint sound of a car starting straight ahead spurred her on. Her tennis shoes pounded the asphalt. Taillights blinked ahead and she stopped, knowing it was a futile chase. With a frustrated slap of her fist against her thigh, she turned and made her way back to her house. She moved back through the trees, walked through her gate and opened her back door. "Mercy, come." The dog didn't need to be told twice. Brooke swept her hand out toward the backyard. "Search." Thirty minutes later, Mercy had come up empty and Brooke was exhausted. She led the way back into the house and called Gavin. "I just had an intruder at my house. Mercy let me know he was there in a tree just over my fence line. When I confronted him, he ran. I tried to chase him down, but I lost him."

"What? You went after him without calling for backup?"

"I didn't have time."

"That wasn't a smart move, Brooke."

She sighed. "What would you have done in my place, Gavin?"

He cleared his throat and didn't speak for a moment. "I'm glad you're all right. Lock your doors and I'll let the local PD know they need to do some frequent drive-bys at your place tonight."

"Great. Thanks."

"You sound tired."

She gave a small laugh. "There's a reason for that. I'm going to bed. See you in the morning."

She hung up with Gavin and walked into her bedroom with Mercy at her heels. "'Night, Mercy. Wake me up if anyone tries anything, will you?"

Mercy settled herself at the end of the bed. Brooke crawled beneath the covers and closed her eyes.

Then opened them. Then got up and locked her bedroom door.

Jonas couldn't sleep and it had nothing to do with the fans sounding like freight trains blowing though his home. Frustration nipped at him. He knew he needed to get some rest, but knowing that and shutting off his mind were two very different things. Hence his vigilance at the front window of his house. He'd left the porch light on in the front and turned on the back lights in case Felix wanted to come in that way. The officer was on the curb. Every so often, he'd get out of his car and do a perimeter scan.

Under police escort, Claire had gone back to the office to take care of the animals. The officer had seen her safely home so at least he didn't have to worry about her or work tonight.

He just had to worry about Felix.

Be anxious for nothing.

The verse ran through his mind. "How do I do that, God? This is Felix we're talking about," he murmured. "Please take care of him, wherever he is."

He wouldn't blame God for not listening, but Jonas figured Brooke was right and God wouldn't hold his absenteeism against him. "Thank You for that," he whispered. But it was time to change that and put God back where He belonged. As a priority. No matter what happened with Felix.

He took another look out the living room window and noticed the police cruiser sitting empty. A shadow disappeared around the corner of the house and he figured the officer was doing another safety check. Jonas had to admit the man was thorough, attentive and alert. Jonas appreciated that.

He glanced at his phone. *Call me, Felix. At least let me know you're all right.* For the first time since his wife had walked out, Jonas felt like letting a few tears flow. He wondered if that made him weak.

Then he wished Brooke were there with him. She wouldn't find him weak; she'd probably offer him her shoulder. He blew out a sigh and shook his head. This was getting him nowhere, but he just couldn't get away from the anxiety clawing at his throat.

He turned away from the window, then stopped and looked back at the police car. The officer hadn't returned yet. Jonas frowned. He'd been watching, hoping to catch Felix walking up the street and as a result, he'd seen the officer come and go over the past two hours.

In all of his patrols around the perimeter of the house, it hadn't taken him this long to return to his car. Uneasiness started to build. Jonas wanted to chalk it up to paranoia, but the events over the past two days wouldn't let him. Had the officer run into trouble? Found something? He picked up his phone and dialed Brooke as he went through the house turning off the loud fans.

"Hello?"

The fact that she answered on the first ring said a lot about her own state of sleeplessness. "Hey, do you have the number for the officer outside my house?"

"No. Why?"

"I've been watching him for the past couple of hours. Well, watching for Felix, but noticing the officer making his rounds around my property. He walked away from his car about ten minutes ago and hasn't come back yet. He's never taken this long."

"Sit tight. I'm on the way."

"What? Why?"

"I'm concerned. I had an intruder—I think. A would-be one anyway. It's possible he went straight from my house to yours. Make sure the doors are locked. I'm on my way and sending backup."

"I don't know if that's necess—" He stopped. A low creak from the front of the house reached his ears. "Wait a minute."

"What is it?" He heard rustling in the background like she was moving, getting ready to leave her house.

"I think someone's in my house," he whispered.

"Get out."

"It could be Felix trying to sneak in." Hope flared. Caution ruled. He wouldn't call out until he knew for sure. He slipped his feet into the loafers he'd left in front of the recliner, then moved to the foot of the stairs. The noise had come from the front of the house, maybe the stairs. Could Felix have crawled through a window? Not likely. Jonas had double-checked them and they'd been locked.

"Jonas? You need to get out of the house until you know for sure who it is."

"What if that's the purpose? Get me out of the house then kill me?" He lowered his voice and looked out at the squad car one more time. Still no sign of the officer. Should he leave? He could make it to the front door. Or should he hide? The feeling of having lived this once before swept over him.

"Good point," Brooke said. "What if you got in your car? Lock the doors and hunker down until help gets there?"

The idea didn't sit well with Jonas. He wanted to confront whoever had the audacity to break into his house with a police car sitting right outside. Then he thought about Felix. What would happen to Felix if Jonas did something stupid and got himself killed?

He went to the back door and looked out into the garage. The moon filtered through the windows and he could make out the shape of his car. He heard Brooke talking in the background. Probably calling for help.

Making up his mind, he opened the door and stepped into the darkness of the garage. He shut the door behind him and glanced back into his kitchen through the glass paned door. Nothing yet.

"Are you there, Jonas?" Brooke asked.

"Yeah," he whispered. He heard the worry in her voice. Where were his keys? In his pants pocket hanging over the chair in his bedroom. He changed into sweats when he'd gotten home.

"What are you doing?"

"Getting out." Standing in his kitchen with his phone pressed to his ear, Jonas saw the shadow of a man, his weapon raised.

"Help's on the way. The officer isn't answering his phone."

Jonas paused only for a second before deciding against hiding in the car. He pressed the garage door and flinched at the low rumble. Would the guy in the kitchen notice? He moved to duck under the door and felt something slam into his back. The concrete rushed up and he threw out an arm to break his fall.

Pain shot up from his wrist to his elbow. He lost a few layers of skin, but figured that was the least of his problems as he rolled to his back only to stare up at the man standing over him, gun trained on his face.

SIXTEEN

Brooke raced through the streets as fast as she dared, siren blaring, lights flashing. Mercy sat in her area in the back, but Brooke could feel the animal's tension reflected in her own. The dog knew something was up and was ready to work.

"Jonas? Are you there? Jonas?" Silence answered her. But he hadn't hung up. "Jonas?"

"Where's the kid?"

Brooke jerked the phone from her ear then shoved it back. "I don't know where he is. We're all looking for him."

"I said where is the kid! Answer me or I'll blow your head off!"

Brooke realized the person wasn't talking to her. He was talking to Jonas and he had a gun on him. Chills swept through her and she pressed the gas a little harder.

"He's missing. He left last night. We're all looking for him." Jonas spoke, his voice low, a thread of steel-laced anger vibrating through the line.

"You're a liar."

"I'm not!" Brooke heard the snarl and prayed he wouldn't do something stupid like attack the guy with the gun. "He got scared and took off. No one knows where he is."

She turned on the road that would lead her to Jonas's house. "Hang on, Jonas."

Through her handset, she heard sirens.

"Let's get out of here!" Another voice.

"What do we do with him?"

"Shoot him."

A gunshot cracked through the line. She flinched and her terror level shot up. There were two of them. And one of them had shot Jonas. "Jonas! No, no no. Please no." A thud and a grunt came through the line. She heard scuffling and running footsteps. "Jonas!" *Oh please, God, don't let him be dead.* She turned the next corner and screeched to a halt in front of Jonas's house. She bolted from the vehicle to find Jonas on the ground, officers chasing two fleeing suspects. Mercy hopped to the ground, her nose working the area around her.

Brooke wanted to take Mercy and follow the officers in pursuit, but her first concern was Jonas. She dropped to her knees beside him and started patting his chest, his arms. "Are you okay? Are you hurt? Where are you shot? You're bleeding!"

He grabbed her hands and sat up. "I'm fine." He glanced at his arm. "That's nothing."

"I heard a gunshot."

"Yeah, but he didn't shoot me." He stood and winced, clasping his injured arm. "One of the officers shot at the guy who had the gun on me. It stopped him long enough so I was able to knock the weapon away from him."

"Did the officer hit him?"

"I don't know."

She nodded to his arm. "You're bleeding," she said again.

"I'm getting used to it." He grunted. "When I came out of the garage, one of them knocked me to the ground. I broke my fall with my arm."

"Is your arm broken?"

"No, just scraped and painful."

She noticed two of the officers who'd been chasing the intruders returning. Their frowns didn't tell a happy ending to the pursuit. She led Jonas over to them. "They got away?" she asked.

"Yeah," the larger officer said. "They had a car waiting. No license plate, but I've got a BOLO for the vehicle. It's a gray Ford Taurus, paint scraped off the right rear bumper."

"How's the officer who was watching the house?" Jonas asked. "I never saw him come back to his car."

"We found him around back. He's out cold. They hit him hard. Ambulance is on the way."

She winced and nodded, then glanced down the street to the right. Then the left. She looked at Jonas. "I think you might be getting to know your neighbors before too long."

He followed her gaze. "At least they don't hide away and ignore trouble in the neighborhood." He shook his head. "They'll probably blackball me from the home owners association."

"Or charge you double dues."

He gave her a tight smile, neither one of them really interested in finding humor in the situation right now. She cupped his chin. "Are you really all right? When I heard that gunshot—" She bit her lip and fought the surge of emotion.

"I'm really all right." He pulled her into a loose hug with his good arm and she pressed her forehead into his chest. She relished the feeling of being in his arms even as she told herself to pull away. He was a case, his son was missing and she had to keep herself at a distance in order to stay objective.

Right.

She looked up to find Nicholas eyeing her with a raised brow. Thankfully he didn't say anything and didn't even give her a funny look.

He did appear concerned. She slipped away from Jonas and put some distance between them so she could think. She gestured to Jonas's arm. "You might need to have that checked."

"By a real doctor?" His lips quirked in a side smile. "Like I did the bullet graze?"

"Touché." She nodded to the house. "Let's get you back inside. I don't think those guys are coming back, but why take chances?"

They made their way back into the house via the front door. Jonas led the way to the den, flipping lights on as he went. The tension in his shoulders was noticeable. Chase and Valor followed behind.

Nicholas looked at Chase. "I think you should stay here. Inside."

Chase nodded. "I was thinking one of us should."

"Brooke's going with me in the morning—" he glanced at his watch "—in a few hours to talk to Congressman Jeffries."

"Then I'll stay," Chase said.

Brooke hesitated. *She* wanted to stay. To make sure that Jonas was all right and that no one tried to break in again. She glanced at Chase. A small smile played around the corners of his mouth and Brooke straightened her spine. “Fine. Sounds good to me.”

She told Mercy to heel and headed out the door, knowing no one bought her nonchalance. She was terrified for Jonas and Felix and knew the others were too. Because as much as she might want to deny it, the old feelings from years past weren’t so old anymore. They were new and exciting and frightening. And if she didn’t find out who was targeting Jonas and Felix, she might be attending funerals, instead of the wedding that kept jumping to the forefront of her mind.

Jonas watched Nicholas and Brooke drive away. He turned to find Chase watching him. Chase’s dog, Valor, sat at his side. The Belgian Malinois yawned and settled his big head on his paws. “Sorry you got babysitting duty,” Jonas said. He went into the kitchen and opened the fridge.

“I’m a former Secret Service agent. I’m used to it.” The man was young, in his midtwenties and tall. His green eyes held life—and a wisdom that came beyond his years. Jonas had a feeling Chase had quite a few stories to tell. “And I don’t mind. It’s different from what I’m usually doing so the change of pace is nice.”

“You said former. Why get out of the Secret Service?”

Chase shrugged. “Search and rescue is my passion. I liked my time in the Secret Service, but when I was offered this position, I jumped at it. This is where I belong.”

Jonas nodded, his mind on his son. It helped having someone there to talk with, but he couldn’t stop wondering if Felix was safe. For the first time, Jonas regretted not getting Felix a phone.

"Are you sure you want to stay here tonight?" Chase asked.

"Yes, Felix may come back home." He looked around. "The worst of the damage was in here. The kitchen and bedrooms are fine now that the smoke is gone. However, I do need to run back to the office and take care of the animals that are there."

"I'll take you."

Jonas nodded. "All right." He looked around the house, the stark emptiness of it slashing his heart. What would he do if Felix never came home? He pulled in a shuddering breath and ordered his mind not to go there. Felix would come home. He had to.

"Someone will find him, Jonas."

He looked into Chase's kind eyes. "Yeah, but will it be the good guys or the bad guys?"

The sun was high overhead when Brooke and Nicholas pulled up to the congressman's front door the next morning. Brooke was breathing a bit easier after the rest of the night passed with no more attempts on Jonas.

The large mansion should have been overbearing and monstrous. And while it was big, it was more classy than ostentatious. At least in Brooke's opinion. That fact probably had to do with the good taste of the congressman's landscaper.

She and Nicholas walked up to the front door, leaving the animals in the well-ventilated vehicle.

Before she could ring the bell, the door opened.

Congressman Jeffries looked impeccable. His gray hair lay slicked back, not a strand daring to be out of place. His blue eyes remained shuttered and his lips didn't curve into a smile. "Come in." He stepped back and Brooke moved inside. Nicholas stayed on her flank and shut the door behind him. "Thank you for seeing us."

"I apologize for all the delays, but they couldn't be helped. I appreciate your understanding." Instead of going into the reasons for those delays, he simply clasped his hands in front of him. "You said you had a few more questions and I'm willing to do whatever it takes to find Michael's killer. You know that."

"Of course, sir."

Congressman Jeffries led them into a formal living area and toward two navy wing-back chairs. "Make yourself comfortable." They did. Jeffries stood near the fireplace and leaned against the massive mantel. "Now, before you start in on your questions, tell me this, has there been any progress on locating my son's killer?"

Brooke shot a look at Nicholas. "No, sir, not much. We do have some things we're working on, but there's no point in talking about them until we see if they're going to pan out."

He frowned, but didn't push the matter. "What kinds of things?"

Brooke pursed her lips and exchanged a glance with Nicholas. He gave a short nod. "Things like a phone that's linked to Rosa Gomez, your late housekeeper."

"What's so important about that?"

"There's a picture on the phone of a man on the cliffs where she died. The picture was taken the day she died so we're looking for him to bring him in and question him." She could give that much information. The man's face was all over the news so the congressman probably already knew that much.

He snorted and waved a hand. "You're right, you don't

have much. What other questions do you have for me then?"

"As you know, we've been looking into everything we possibly can to figure out who would have something against you."

"Yes."

"It seems you and Thorn Industries have a rather close relationship," Nicholas said. He kept his tone mild, but Brooke heard the thread of steel beneath the words.

"What are you implying?" Jeffries asked, eyes flashing.

Brooke opened her mouth, but Nicholas beat her to it. "I'm not implying anything. I'm simply curious about the two bills you introduced that were subsequently passed."

Jeffries's lips tightened.

Brooke picked up when the man didn't speak. "We found it very interesting that those bills allowed Thorn Industries to keep manufacturing a drug with dangerous side effects. And of course that puts more money in your pocket."

"How dare you?" The congressman took a step toward Nicholas, fists clenched at his side, face red.

Nicholas tensed, but Brooke simply watched the man, then said, "We dare because these are facts, sir. Did Michael find out what you were doing? What you were supporting? Did Michael threaten to expose you? Did you get so desperate to keep your secrets that you had to kill your own son?"

Congressman Jeffries gaped at her. Even Nicholas looked a bit stunned at her lack of finesse. But Brooke did it for a reason. She waited for Jeffries's reaction.

And wasn't disappointed.

His red face turned purple. "Unbelievable. My son

is dead! Whoever shot him shot me, too. And you dare come into my home and accuse me of killing Michael? Get out. Both of you!"

Nicholas shifted. Brooke met the man's eyes. "Not until you tell us about Thorn Industries. We can keep digging, of course, but if you'll just tell us what we need to know then that'll make things move along a little faster. Which is what you want, right?"

His nostrils flared and the color in his face stayed high, but he gave a short nod. It took him a moment to get his breathing under control. He finally drew in a deep breath and closed his eyes. When he opened them, hard chips of ice stared at her. "Fine. Thorn Industries tried to bribe me in passing the bill. I would never do that. I wouldn't jeopardize my career, my livelihood or my reputation. That would be political suicide."

"Yes, sir, that's true."

"So I told them no. I refused." He gave a halfhearted laugh. "I play by the rules and get accused of murder." The hardness melted. Tears filled his eyes, his shoulders slumped and he dropped to the couch to lower his head to his hands. Sobs shook his shoulders.

Brooke swallowed. Had she gone too far? She raised an eyebrow at Nicholas and he shrugged.

"Sir?" Brooke asked.

He hiccupped and pulled a tissue from the box on the end table. He wiped his face. "I'm sorry. So sorry. But I just miss Michael so much. And your questions..."

Brooke cleared her throat. "Yes, well, I apologize. Sometimes my tongue gets ahead of my brain."

The man nodded. "I miss my son," he whispered.

"Of course you do. I'm sorry for the hard questions. We're just trying to find who did this."

He sniffled and grabbed another handful of tissues. "I know. I know. Michael was a good man. He was a bit of a do-gooder crusader, you know. Nothing set him off like finding out someone was corrupt in the government." He looked up. "That was his big thing. He fought against government corruption." He sighed. "And he didn't care who he made mad. He took on anyone he thought needed taking down or exposed. Anyone." He blew his nose and wiped his eyes. His gaze jumped from Nicholas's to Brooke's. "And because of that, he was killed. No, I don't have proof, but I don't need it. I just know it."

The tears continued to leak down his face. Nicholas stood and Brooke followed his example, her lips pulled into a frown. Nicholas grabbed more tissues and pushed them into Jeffries's hand. "I'm sorry, sir. We'll leave now, but please call us if there's anything else you can think of."

The tears had stopped, but Brooke couldn't deny the agony in the man's eyes. Shame flickered and she had to work to suppress it.

"Of course I'll call," Jeffries said. He swallowed and drew in another shuddering breath. "I appreciate everything you're doing. I know you're working hard. Forgive me for being bullheaded. I just want the people responsible for Michael's death to be brought to justice."

"We do, too, sir," Brooke said. "We do, too."

She and Nicholas left and stood in front of their vehicles. Brooke's phone buzzed and she glanced at the text. "Jonas is at work. Chase is still with him and there's a patrol car in the parking lot."

"Good. He's covered." Nicholas nodded. "Wish we could find his son."

"That makes two of us."

Her phone buzzed again. "It's Gavin."

"Take it."

She nodded and lifted the phone to her ear. "Hi, Gavin."

"Brooke. We need you and Mercy to head over to Brothers Jewelry Store. There's been a break-in at their downtown store. One of the robbers left behind a glove. DC police asked for K-9 help because of the glove. We want to see if Mercy can track down anything else that might give us a clue who these guys are."

"We're on our way."

Brooke raced to her vehicle, her suspicions about the congressman not satisfied; however, there was nothing to do but head to the other case. Nicholas would write up the conversation word for word and they could discuss it at the next Capitol K-9 meeting. Gavin would be furious with her.

Ten minutes later, she pulled into the parking lot of the jewelry store. An array of law enforcement was already in action. She flashed her badge and Mercy quivered at her side, ready to work.

An officer approached her. "Hey, Brooke."

"Hey, Elizabeth. They've got you out here, too?" Elizabeth Carter, another one of the Capitol K-9 team members. Her border collie, Buddy, sat at her side.

Elizabeth nodded.

"Anyone hurt?" Brooke asked.

"The guard. He was shot in the chest. It's touch and go right now."

Brooke winced. "Okay, where's the glove?"

"The lead detective has it." She rubbed Buddy's ears. "Let's go, boy."

They took off and Brooke turned to find herself face-to-face with Detective David Delvecchio. “You the lead?”

“I am.”

“Then let’s go.”

He held a rubber glove out to her. She popped it over her hand and reached into the paper bag he had in his other hand. Holding the leather glove between two fingers, she let Mercy get a good sniff. The dog’s nose wiggled. “Seek.”

Mercy took off like a shot to the edge of the road. Brooke followed her at a fast trot, the detective staying with her. “You got this call, huh?” he asked. “They take you off the other case?”

“Of course not. I’m just like you. I work more than one case at a time.”

Mercy stopped, went to the edge of the road and into the trees.

“She any good?” David asked.

“One of the best.” He glanced at her then back at the dog. “Mercy can find evidence that’s left behind. Her nose is super sensitive.”

“I know how the dogs work.”

“Right.” He might think he knew, but Brooke had a feeling he didn’t know details. Mercy sifted through the scents all around them and found the one that didn’t fit.

“Sorry. I know how they work. I’m not used to working with them, that’s all,” the detective said.

“It’s fine.”

Mercy paced, then sat and looked back. Brooke went to her and rubbed her ears. “Good girl.”

“What did she find?”

“You have an evidence bag?”

He handed one to her.

With her gloved hand, she reached out and picked up the evidence Mercy had focused on. "It's a pearl earring."

"They came this way then."

"Yes."

"If it was them."

"It was. If the earring had been out here for an extended period of time, its scent would have blended with the surroundings. The fact that she picked up on a scent that doesn't belong says the earring is a new addition to the area."

The detective patted Mercy's head. "Well, you're a good one." Mercy rewarded his praise with a tongue swipe to the hand. Detective Delvecchio looked startled, then laughed. Brooke handed him a bottle of hand sanitizer without a word. He used it and handed it back to her. She smiled.

They made their way back to the road. Brooke led the way, Mercy at her left, the detective on her right. Mercy gave a sudden yelping cry and sat, her paw lifted. Brooke spun. "What is it?"

"What happened to her?" the detective asked.

"I don't know." Mercy held her paw away from the ground and refused to stand. Brooke dropped to her knees. "What did you step on, girl?"

Brooke took the dog's paw in her hand and tried to see, but Mercy kept pulling it away from her. She sighed. "Well, I guess we're going to see Jonas a lot sooner than we'd planned."

In spite of her worry over Mercy, the thought lifted her spirits higher than they'd been all day.

SEVENTEEN

Jonas stood at the window waiting. Brooke had called and said Mercy had been hurt and he'd told her to bring the dog in. His imagination took flight. Had she been shot protecting Brooke? Had Brooke been in danger? His breath whooshed out when Brooke turned in to the parking lot of the office. She flashed her badge at the officers and they waved her in.

Clients had come and gone all morning, eyes wide, curiosity eating at them. Jonas had been vague in his answers to their questions.

Brooke stepped from the vehicle then opened the back door. She lifted Mercy into her arms and staggered slightly under the dog's weight. Jonas went to help, but the officer motioned him back. "We don't want you out here. You'd be too exposed."

Jonas chafed at the constraints. "Then help her with the dog."

The larger officer, who stood about six feet two, took Mercy from Brooke.

"Thanks," she told him.

"Bring her back here," Jonas said.

The officer carried Mercy with ease and gently laid her on the examination table, then left them alone in the room.

Jonas looked at Brooke. "What happened to her?"

"I think she stepped on something. Either that or she got stung by a bee or—" She shrugged. "I don't know. I didn't think it was that serious, but she wouldn't let me look at it."

Jonas reached for the paw that the animal favored. Mercy whined and pulled away from him. He frowned. "I'm going to have to sedate her."

Brooke sighed. "Fine. She's not going to let you touch her without it, I'm afraid."

He patted the dog's head. "I'll be back in a minute and we'll get you all fixed up."

"Where's Claire?"

He paused at the door. "I told her not to come in today. I just didn't want her in the middle of all the craziness."

"You've been handling the office by yourself all morning?"

"Yes." He gave her a weary smile.

"No wonder you look beat."

"Thanks."

She grabbed his hand. "No. I need to thank you."

"It's my pleasure. I'll be right back."

Brooke let him go this time.

When he returned he had a syringe. Brooke held the dog while Jonas administered the medicine. He noticed her tenderness with her friend, her partner. He also noticed Brooke smelled good. Really good in spite of whatever work she'd been doing.

Soon the drug took effect. Mercy leaned heavily against Brooke and Jonas had to curb his jealousy. He shook his head. Jealous of a dog? He was being ridiculous. "My wife didn't like animals."

Brooke stilled. "Is that why you don't have one at your home?"

"Part of the reason."

"And the other part?"

He sighed. He'd opened the door to the topic, he supposed he'd walk through it. "I didn't want anything to compete with the time I needed to spend with Felix."

"And taking care of an animal would keep you from spending time with your son?"

"I thought it might."

"Or it might bring you closer together."

He glanced up. "Maybe."

"Come on, Jonas, you saw him with those puppies. He was great."

"I know." He did know. "It's something to think about for sure. When he comes home."

"Which is going to be soon."

He shook his head, worry consuming him once again. "I've put him in God's hands."

"No better place for him to be."

"Unfortunately, I keep taking him back, convinced that I can do a better job than God when it comes to Felix." He sighed. "I know that's not true, I've just got to live like I believe it." He nodded at Mercy. "I think I'll be able to take a look now."

Mercy's eyes were closed and a light snore slipped from her. He leaned in to get a closer look at the animal's wounded paw. "Aha."

"What is it?"

"It's not a thorn or a bee sting, but just as painful." He reached for a pair of tweezers, pulled a magnifying glass down over his eye and gently pulled a sliver of glass from Mercy's paw. The dog didn't even move. Jonas held up the piece of glass. "No wonder she was in pain and didn't want to put weight on that foot."

Brooke laid the dog on the table and stroked her head. Mercy stirred enough to give Brooke's hand a lick, then fell back into a doze. Jonas threw the glass in the trash. "I'll clean it and take a stitch. She'll be all right in a day or two."

"I'm glad it was something so simple."

"Yeah. We haven't had much of simple lately."

Twenty minutes later, Jonas had Mercy settled on a blanket in a kennel at the back of the office. He shut the door. "She'll sleep it off and be ready to go in the morning."

"Thanks so much, Jonas."

He looked into her grateful eyes and felt his heart flip over. He curled his fingers into a fist to keep from reaching out to her. Not yet. Not while Felix's whereabouts were still up in the air.

She bit her lip and turned away as though reading his thoughts. "I'll let Gavin know what's happened." She glanced at her watch. "I probably need to get back to my office and get some paperwork done or I'll be spending the night there."

"Go on. I'll take care of Mercy."

"I know you will."

His phone rang as she gathered her things. "Hello?"

"Dr. Parker, this is Officer Davenport. We were patrolling past your house and noticed your front door open."

"What?" he snapped.

At his sharp tone, Brooke looked at him. He told her what the officer said.

She frowned. "Ask him if someone is inside?"

He repeated the question to the officer. "No, sir. We swept the place, but you might want to come home and see if anything's missing."

"I'll be right there."

Brooke drove with precision and one eye on the rear-view mirror. Leaving Mercy behind felt like she'd just cut off her right arm, but the drugged dog would be much more comfortable sleeping it off in the kennel than being transported in the back of the car.

Jonas rode beside her, his heavy frown and brooding eyes reflecting his inner turmoil. "I need to be searching for my son."

"We're looking for him, Jonas. What do you think you could do that the cops aren't doing?"

He shook his head and blew out a harsh sigh. "I don't know. Something. I can't believe he could just disappear like that."

He could disappear like that if he were dead. Brooke kept her eyes on the road and her thoughts to herself. But the more time passed with no word about the teen, the more her mind went to dark places. "Did you try calling his friends again?"

"Yes. I'm sure a couple of the parents think Felix is just a runaway." He tapped his fingers against his thigh. "And I believe he did leave on his own."

"The security video confirms that."

He nodded. "But that doesn't mean he doesn't need help."

"I agree. I think he needs help more than ever right now."

"I'm scared to death the wrong people are going to find him."

"I know." She turned in to his drive. The front door still stood cracked open and Brooke could see someone standing just inside. The person peered out, then stepped onto the porch. Brooke figured it was the officer whose empty squad car sat on the curb. He motioned them in and Jonas bolted from the vehicle. Brooke stayed right behind him, her nerves stretched tight. Would they never catch a break?

She followed Jonas through the front door and the officer shut it behind them. "Okay, we've gone through the house and found nothing damaged, no electronics obviously missing, but we need you to walk through and see if there's anything small that's been taken, anything that I wouldn't notice."

Jonas rubbed a hand down his face. Brooke noticed the smoky smell had faded almost completely, the big fans left by the restoration company having done their job.

Jonas walked through the house and Brooke stayed behind him. "See anything missing or just not right?"

"Not so far."

They passed through the den, toured the kitchen, then back into the foyer and up the stairs to the master bedroom. She waited outside the room, but couldn't help a curious glance inside. Large oak furniture, dark browns and beiges and a few red throw pillows on the perfectly made-up bed. Dark curtains and black rug on the floor. It definitely needed a woman's touch and Brooke already had it redecorated by the time he joined her in the hall.

She gulped and ordered herself to focus on the task at hand. "Nothing?"

"No." He slipped past her and into Felix's room. It

looked the same as it had the last she'd been in here. Jonas simply stood in the doorway and looked. She watched him scan the room.

And frown.

"What is it?" she asked.

"There was a sweatshirt tossed over the back of his footboard. Next to the jeans and hoodie." He picked them up then set it back where he found it.

"How do you know the sweatshirt's missing?"

"Because I put it there."

"Maybe Felix moved it?"

He shook his head. "No, he hasn't been back in his room since we moved over to the office. I grabbed some clothes for him after the whole Molotov cocktail and smoke explosion, but it wasn't that sweatshirt and Felix hasn't been here." He rubbed his chin. "Do you have pictures of his room? A cop took pictures the night of the break-in."

"Fiona will have them. She has everything related to the case." Brooke pulled her cell phone from her pocket and hit Fiona's speed dial number.

"Yes, ma'am?"

"Hey, I need the pictures from the Parker scene."

"Coming your way. Any pictures in particular?"

"The ones of the teenager's bed and the clothes on it."

"Check your phone in about two minutes."

"Thanks, Fiona."

"Anytime."

Brooke hung up and waited. Less than the promised two minutes later, it buzzed. She pulled up the pictures and Jonas leaned over her shoulder to see. Her awareness meter shot to the top level. His breath brushed her ear and she swallowed. Why did he affect her so? Even more so than the first time she'd seen him again. Had that just been a couple of days? It felt as though they were picking up right where they'd left off. She shivered and he rested a hand on her shoulder.

"You okay?" he asked.

"I'm fine." She scrolled through the photos, noting the slight tremble in her fingers. She hoped Jonas didn't notice.

"There," he said.

She stopped. "That one?" She pointed to the blue sweatshirt draped over the foot of the bed. Next to a pair of jeans and a gray hoodie. Just like Jonas said.

"That's it. It's missing."

"So while you were at work and the police coverage on your house was minimal, someone snuck in and stole the sweatshirt. Why?"

"Maybe Felix was cold and had one of his friends steal it." He rubbed a hand down his face. "I don't know."

"Or he came back and got it himself."

"I hope so, I pray he did," Jonas said.

It would mean he was moving under his own steam, that he wasn't being held captive somewhere. "You know, the fact that there's been no ransom demand, that's a good thing. If the people who want the phone knew Felix was missing, even if they didn't have him, they might act like they did and demand you give him the phone."

"Or he told them he handed it over to the police and doesn't have it anymore and they have no use for him so they—" He bit his lip and turned away.

Brooke grimaced. She'd thought of that scenario, she just hadn't wanted to say it out loud. "Just in case, let's not let on that Felix doesn't have the phone anymore. I was going to suggest a press conference to announce that the phone had been found and was in the unit's possession, but now I don't think that's a good idea. Not yet. Not until we find Felix and make sure he's not using the fact that he had the phone as a way to stay alive until help can get to him."

Jonas nodded, a sick look on his face. "What if he's already told them he doesn't have it?"

Brooke blew out a long sigh. "Then he might be in serious trouble."

EIGHTEEN

Early the next morning, Jonas hung up with Nicholas after getting an update on the search for Felix. Nothing yet. He turned to grab his jacket when his phone rang for the second time in ten minutes. He glanced at the caller ID, praying for a number he didn't recognize. An unfamiliar number might mean Felix had found or borrowed a phone and decided to call.

But he knew the number and his hopes plummeted. "Hi, Claire."

"I'm happy to hear your voice, too."

He winced. "Sorry. I was hoping you were Felix."

"Of course you were." Her voice softened and sympathy flowed through the line. "I'm sorry."

"No problem."

"Have you heard anything about him? Has anyone found anything at all that might indicate where he is?"

"No, but the officers were out looking all night and I'm staying right by my phone in case he calls again." He sighed. "I was just getting ready to head to the office. Are you already there?"

"I came in. I can't sit at home doing nothing, you know that."

"I know. I don't know what I'd do without you. All right. Is there an officer in sight?"

"Yes. Two of them. Parked right out front. They got here about the same time I did."

"Good. You should be safe enough, then. I'll see you in a few minutes."

He hung up with Claire and started gathering his wallet and keys when he remembered Chase was probably in his kitchen. Jonas descended the steps and found the man sitting at the kitchen table sipping a cup of coffee. "Morning," he said.

Jonas nodded. "Morning."

Chase hefted the mug. "Hope you don't mind."

"Are you kidding? You can help yourself to anything you need or want. I can't tell you how much I appreciate all you guys are doing to find Felix and keep me safe."

Chase's expression relaxed a fraction. "You're welcome. We've had guys out all night looking for him. They want a good ending to this story, too."

"I know. And I know it's probably just all in a day's work for you, but—" He shrugged and grabbed his silver travel mug from the sink. After he filled it with the black brew, he took a sip and breathed in a grateful breath.

A knock on his door pulled Chase from his chair. His hand went to his weapon and he started for the door. "Brooke said she'd come get you this morning, so it's probably her, but we don't need to take any chances."

Tension threaded across Jonas's shoulders. He was ready for this to be over, for his son to be home. To catch whoever was causing the problems and get this burden off his shoulders.

"It's me," Brooke said.

Jonas shifted and set his cup on the counter. Brooke

walked into the kitchen and their eyes met. As always, that special zing whipped through him. He blinked and waved to the coffeepot. "Chase was the hero this morning. May I offer you a cup?"

"Sure."

He filled her cup and handed it to her. "Are you ready to go see Mercy?"

"Absolutely."

"Claire called me. She's there now."

Chase stepped to the door. "I'm going to head back to the office. Let me know if you need anything else."

"Thanks."

Jonas grabbed his keys and headed out after Chase.

"Hey, wait up," Brooke called.

Jonas turned. Brooke was on his heels, holding out his phone. He took it from her with a crooked smile. "I guess I'm a little distracted these days."

"You think?"

Jonas went to his vehicle.

Brooke bypassed him. "Go back on the porch and wait, will you?"

Jonas frowned. "Why?"

"I want to check the car."

Her meaning dawned. "You think someone planted a bomb in my car?"

"I don't know. That's why I'm checking."

Jonas stood on the porch, one hand cramped around his phone, the other around his cup. A bomb? The thought had never occurred to him. He watched her cover the car bumper to bumper. She'd even pulled out a small mirror to check the undercarriage.

Finally she pushed herself up off the concrete drive and held out a hand. "Toss me your keys, will you?"

Jonas narrowed his eyes. "So you can start it and see if it blows up?"

Brooke laughed. "I'm relatively sure it's safe. I don't have a death wish."

"Then I'll start it myself."

"Jonas."

He stepped around her. "No way." He opened the door and tossed his stuff inside and slid into the driver's seat.

Brooke crossed her arms and glared at him.

Jonas met her glare for glare. "Are you sure this thing's not going to blow?"

She sighed. "Yes. I didn't see anything to indicate a bomb. Nothing under the car, nothing under the hood. I'm willing to put the key in the ignition and start the car."

"Then I trust you." Without hesitation he inserted the key and turned it. The car started with a low growl and he realized he still held his breath.

Brooke shook her head and went to her own vehicle. She climbed in and motioned for him to go ahead. He pulled around her and drove the short mile and a half to his office. When he arrived at the parking lot, he noted the police officers and offered a short wave.

Brooke parked and climbed from the vehicle. He could see her tapping her hand on her thigh while she waited on him. She wanted to see her dog and couldn't quite hide her impatience. He led the way into the office, noting she scanned the area in spite of the police coverage. Nothing must have set off her internal alarm. She stepped inside and he shut the door just as Claire came from the back, her brow furrowed.

"What is it?" Jonas asked.

"You didn't turn the alarm system on when you left last night."

"Of course I did."

The woman's frown deepened. "It wasn't on when I got here."

Jonas went to the panel. It was dark.

"Did you leave one of the cages open last night?" Claire asked.

Jonas turned, a ball of dread forming in his midsection. "No, of course not. Why?"

"Because I think one of the animals is missing."

"Which one?" The dread blew up into outright fear as he rushed through the door to the kennel. Brooke stayed right behind. He came to a stop at the open cage.

"Mercy," Brooke whispered. "She's gone."

Brooke blinked, then blinked again as though the act would change the facts. The cage was still empty. "Someone stole her."

"That's impossible," Jonas snapped. "I remember activating the alarm system when I left yesterday. After all the crazy stuff going on, there's no way I would forget that."

Brooke believed him. She spun to find one of the officers behind her. "Can you check the alarm system?"

"Of course." He left and Brooke turned back to Jonas. "This is crazy. Why would someone steal Mercy? It's not like she can tell them what she knows." She couldn't help the sarcasm.

He still looked stunned. And angry. He'd just about reached his breaking point and she didn't blame him. She was pretty mad herself and terribly worried about Mercy. Now she had to track down a missing teen and a stolen dog. She pulled in a deep breath and pinched the bridge of her nose. "All right. I need to think for a minute. And call Gavin." She pulled out her phone as the officer stepped back inside.

"Whoever it was is a professional. The box cover was unscrewed, the phone wire cut first, then the alarm wires cut and the cover replaced. Just to look at it you'd never know anything was wrong."

Jonas reached across the desk, grabbed the phone and pressed it to his ear. "Dead." He slammed it down.

Claire gasped. "I didn't even pick the phone up this morning. I saw the alarm was off and thought you must not have turned it on when you left. I was just going to read you the riot act and—" She pressed her fingers to her lips. "I'm sorry."

"It's not your fault, Claire. Don't beat yourself up about it."

"But—"

"I mean it. Really, I think you should go home and stay there until this is all resolved. I'm going to call my clients and refer them to another vet."

Claire and Brooke gasped in unison. "Jonas, your business will go under," Brooke said.

"Right now, I can't worry about this practice. Mercy is missing. Someone is trying to kill me. I have to find my son." He looked at Claire. "And I don't want to risk putting you in danger just because you happen to work for me."

Claire's gaze bounced between Brooke and Jonas before she finally sighed. "Okay. You're probably right." She bit her lip. "But will you stay in touch? Let me know you're all right and when you find Felix?"

"Of course." Jonas escorted her to the door and Brooke dialed Gavin's number. Her heart was heavy. For Jonas and Felix and for Mercy. Please, God, don't let them hurt any of them. She knew why they wanted Felix—they thought he might still have the phone. That and they thought he could ID the guy he saw in the woods. But why would they take Mercy?

Gavin answered and Brooke drew in a deep breath. "Mercy's been stolen."

"What?" His shout made her flinch, but she didn't back away.

"Someone broke into Jonas's practice last night and took her right out of the cage."

"Any video?"

"No. The wires were cut. Telephone, video cameras, everything."

"Of course they were."

She could almost picture him pacing the floor of his office.

"You've got to find her, Brooke."

"I know. If she can get away from whoever has her, she'll find her way home, but if they've got her tied up somewhere..."

"Okay, we'll put out a BOLO on her. Get her picture on the news and all that. I'll also have Fiona work any angles she might have in tracking Mercy. She has the GPS on her collar. Hold on one second." Brooke held. She heard Gavin shout for Fiona. He came back on the line. "Okay, Fiona's on the computer right now."

Brooke paced from one end of the room to the other. "Anything?"

"Not yet."

Brooke paced another route. "Well?"

"Working on it, Brooke. Fiona?"

"Nothing like a little bit of impatience," she heard the woman say. Brooke pictured her in a pink flowing skirt, matching Hawaiian shirt with pink flowers, her hair pulled up on her head and held in place with her glasses. "Brooke?"

"Yes, Fiona."

"I can't track Mercy, I'm sorry. The GPS unit on her collar has been removed."

Brooke groaned then pulled herself together. "All right. What now?"

"I want to have a meeting. Let's assemble the team, but tell Nicholas to stay on Jonas. I don't want him unprotected," Gavin said.

"I'll do that as soon as we hang up."

"Hanging up now."

She dialed Nicholas. He answered with a gruff hello. "Hey, I need some more help. Do you think Margaret would release you one more time?"

Gavin was the captain and in charge of the investigation, but Margaret was Gavin's boss and had the final say in where Nicholas was assigned.

"If it's related to catching Michael Jeffries's killer, I think I pretty much have carte blanche."

"Great." She updated him about Mercy and her need to leave. "If you can cover Jonas, I'll work on finding Mercy."

"I'm on the way."

"Thank you." She stopped and thought. "Okay, here's the plan. I'm going to run by my house and make sure Mercy isn't wandering around there. If she got away, that's the first place she'd go."

"Do that. I'll take care of Jonas and see you at the office soon after."

Brooke hung up and told Jonas, "I'm going by my

house then on to the meeting. I'll check in with you after. Please text me and let me know if you find Felix."

"Of course," Jonas said.

His anxiety and worry grabbed at her and she just prayed that Jonas or one of the officers found him before anyone else. Because if the good guys didn't find him soon, she had a sinking feeling the bad guys would.

NINETEEN

Jonas watched Nicholas and Brooke exchange a few brief words before she climbed into her SUV and pulled into the street. He said a short prayer for her safety and another for Felix and Mercy.

Jonas swung the door open for him and Nicholas stepped inside. "How are you doing?"

"Hanging in there. Still no word from Felix and now Mercy's missing."

Jonas led Nicholas into the break room and pulled two sodas from the refrigerator. He tossed one to Nicholas, who caught it midair. "Thanks."

"Sure. So what's next?"

Nicholas took a swig and sat in the nearest chair. "We keep digging, keep looking for Felix and searching for a way to outsmart the bad guys and catch them."

They discussed different strategies and possibilities for the next several minutes. The phone rang and Jonas went to answer it. When he returned, he found Nicholas hanging up. "We got a sighting on your son," he said.

Jonas's breath whooshed from his lungs. "Where?"

"Over off Hilton Street."

Jonas frowned. "That's near his friend Travis's house. One street over, I believe."

Nicholas lifted a brow. "You think Travis's been hiding him all this time?"

"I don't know, but I'm going to find out." He grabbed his keys. "Who spotted him?"

"One of the patrol officers. He called for him by name and the boy turned so he feels like it's definitely Felix."

Jonas headed for the door.

"Hold on a second. I'll drive."

"And I'll call Brooke." Jonas donned his vest under Nicholas's watchful eye, then dialed Brooke's number on his way to the vehicle. Her phone went to voice mail for the next two times he tried to call. "She's not answering."

"We'll keep trying."

Throughout the ride to the Fuller home, Jonas dialed Brooke's number. The fact that she wasn't answering concerned him.

"Maybe she found Mercy and is getting help. We'll call her again as soon as we leave here."

When they arrived at the Fuller home, Jonas climbed from the vehicle with Nicholas right behind him. He walked up to the front door and rang the bell. No one answered. He'd called the school to check and see if Felix had shown up, but he was reported as being absent. Travis was also absent. Jonas wasn't surprised.

No one answered the door. He turned to Nicholas. "The parents are probably at work."

"Do you have a number?"

"I have cell phones, not work numbers."

"Let's try them."

Jonas dialed the first number and paced while the

phone rang. Just when the thought it might go to voice mail, Charles Fuller answered. "Charles, this is Jonas Parker."

"How are you? Have you found Felix?"

"No, no, we haven't. I'm at your house right now, though. He was spotted not too far from here. Did you know Travis wasn't in school today?"

"What? I dropped him off this morning myself. What do you mean he's not in school?"

Jonas winced at the man's shout. He didn't blame him, though. "I think the boys may be together. If so, we need to find them."

"Does this have to do with all of the trouble you've been having?"

"You know about it?"

"Just what Claire's shared with my wife."

Jonas grimaced. Claire and Hilary Fuller had become friends when she'd brought the Fuller's cat into the office during Jonas's first week of practice. He knew they regularly met for lunch. He shouldn't be surprised Claire would confide in her friend.

"Do I need to come home?"

"No, but do you know where the boys might go to hang out and try not to be spotted?"

Charles paused, then sighed. "No, I can't think of anyplace. Travis doesn't say much. He has his phone with him, I'll give him a call. You can hold this line while I call on another."

"Thanks."

Jonas waited. He glanced at his watch, his impatience building. Finally, he heard the phone click. "Jonas?"

"Yeah."

"He's not answering, but I have software on my computer at home that will allow me to track his phone. I'll be there shortly."

He looked at Nicholas. "Just give me the number, I have a feeling I can get it tracked faster than you."

The man paused for a second, then rattled off the number. Jonas related it to Nicholas and the man got on his phone. He heard him asking for someone named Fiona. "Thanks, Charles."

"I'm on my way home. I'll help you look for the boys."

And pray they found them before the bad guys did.

Brooke drove to her house, praying for Felix, Jonas and Mercy. She pulled into her drive and got out of her car. "Mercy? Girl? Are you here?"

The dog didn't come out from under any of the shrubbery lining the front of her house. Brooke decided to do a perimeter search and walked to the edge of the property then down the side of the house. "Mercy? You here?"

Again no sign.

She had a feeling the search was in vain, but she had to look around the entire area before she would be satisfied. She continued to the back and wound up at the trees lining the back fence. She couldn't help looking up, searching the trees, remembering how easy it had been for someone to climb one and look down into her backyard. She shuddered and moved on until she circled back to her car. With a sigh and a heavy heart, she realized Mercy was either too far away to find her way home or she was unable to get away from whoever took her. Or both.

Brooke decided to make one more pass and check the

backyard. She didn't see how Mercy could have gotten into it, but the dog was clever. Brooke opened her front door, stepped inside and shut it behind her. She walked through to the kitchen then pushed open the door that led to the yard. "Mercy?"

Nothing.

Brooke finally decided to give it up. The dog wasn't here. She reached for her phone to call Gavin and grimaced when her hand landed on her empty clip. She must have left the device in her car in her haste to check for Mercy. She stood on the porch for just a moment, thinking. They'd stolen Mercy. They'd stolen Felix's sweatshirt. Why? The two were connected and her mind immediately put it together. They wanted Mercy to track Felix. Of course. She couldn't believe it hadn't clicked sooner. She had to call Gavin. And Jonas.

Brooke stepped back inside the house and reached for the kitchen wall phone. And stopped. Smoke? Not something-on-fire smoke. Cigarette smoke. Stale cigarette smoke.

Someone was in her house?

Her brain scrambled. Had she locked the front door behind her?

No.

She spun, had a flash of something moving toward her head. Blinding pain.

Then blackness.

Jonas, Charles Fuller and Nicholas searched the house from top to bottom with no sign of the boys. They covered the yard area and several officers cruised nearby streets. Jonas prayed one of the officers spotted Felix or found someone who'd seen him. They returned to the house to wait. Max stayed by Nicholas's side, his intelligent brown eyes never straying from his partner.

Jonas looked at the dog, then at Nicholas. "You know, it's highly likely that if Travis is helping Felix out today, he's been helping hide him all along."

Nicholas scratched Max's ears and nodded. "I was thinking the same thing." He looked at Charles. "Do you have something of Travis's that Max can sniff? Then I can turn him loose and see what he comes up with."

"Of course." Charles disappeared down the hall, then came back with a blue sweatshirt. Nicholas took it and held it out to Max who nosed it. He huffed and snuffled it one more time, then lifted his head.

"I'll take him outside since we know the boys aren't in here. Hopefully, he'll catch the scent and take us on a walk."

Jonas stared. "That's why."

"What?" Nicholas turned.

"That's why they stole Felix's sweatshirt and Mercy. They want to use Mercy to find Felix." He lifted his gaze to lock it on the other officer's. "I've got to get in touch with Brooke."

Brooke rolled and groaned. Something kept nudging her in the ribs while little people drummed on her brain. She winced and tried to sit up, but found she couldn't do it. Her head lay on something hard. She pulled her eyes open, trying to figure out what truck had hit her. The flu? The ringing in her ears finally stopped then started up again.

She blinked. Then blinked again. The fog hovering

over her mind lifted when she saw the black-booted feet in front of her face. Squinting against the raging headache and the sudden burst of nausea, she drew in a steadying breath as the memory rushed in. She'd come looking for Mercy. Someone had been waiting on her and caught her off guard.

"You awake?" a gruff voice asked.

She closed her eyes, praying, trying to move her hands. Something held them together. Duct tape? At least they were in front of her. She moved her feet. Not bound.

A harder kick to the ribs. She gasped, opened her eyes and cried out at the excruciating pain that lanced through her head. The room spun, the darkness beckoned.

"Yeah," the voice said. "That's what I thought. Don't pass out on me again or I'll just shoot you and move on. I need information and can't get it if you're unconscious."

Brooke didn't move, didn't breathe. The pain eased a bit and she tried opening her eyes once more. Her gaze landed on her attacker and her training kicked in. Midthirties, strong, sleeveless muscle shirt, tattoo of a scorpion on his right shoulder. A year-round tan, five-o'clock shadow.

The man from the vet's office.

The man Felix had seen on the cliffs.

The man who'd been trying to kill them to get to the phone. "Can't get it if I'm dead either." A spark of something flashed in his dark eyes. Admiration? More likely annoyance. "If you want information, I suggest you quit hitting me," she rasped.

"Guess you got a bit of a headache, huh?"

"A bit."

He moved his weapon about an inch from her nose.

"I hit you a little harder than I meant to, but don't worry, it's going to quit hurting real soon."

Fear flickered, but she made sure it didn't show. "What do you want?" she asked.

"The phone."

As he spit the two words, she heard the ringing again and realized it was her cell phone. Not exactly the one he was after. He didn't know that one had been turned over to the Capitol K-9 team. She studied him as she waited for another round of nausea to pass. "I don't have it. Haven't you figured that out by now?"

The man spat. "But you can get it."

"Who killed Michael Jeffries?"

"Wouldn't you like to know?" He laughed and seemed genuinely amused. Brooke tugged at her hands, trying to be subtle, but needing to know how strong and well wrapped the tape was. Another tug. Her hope took a nosedive. She'd need some time to work her way out of the tape. And by the look in his eyes, time was something she didn't have. He shoved the weapon closer. "Now. Where's the phone?"

Jonas kept dialing Brooke's number. And it kept going to voice mail after the fourth ring. Why wasn't she answering? Nicholas seemed concerned as well when she didn't pick up his call either. "I'm calling Gavin."

"I'm going to Brooke's house. She said she was going to check and see if Mercy had come home before going to the meeting with your boss."

"I'll drive," Nicholas said.

They climbed into the vehicle and Max settled himself in his designated area in the kennel. Nicholas shut the door. Worry pinched Jonas and he tried her number once again. He hung up on the voice mail.

Nicholas called his boss and Jonas listened to the conversation. "Brooke's not answering her phone. Is she already with you?" Nicholas looked at Jonas and shook his head. Brooke wasn't there.

Nicholas drove quickly and efficiently, his eyes focused on the road and on his task. Jonas watched the clock. They weren't that far away, but if Brooke was in trouble, every second might count.

"Gavin's sending backup," Nicholas said as he took the next left.

"Will they beat us there?"

"Not likely."

They slowed in front of Brooke's house. Jonas had his door open before Nicholas pulled to a stop. He raced to the front door, then stopped and took a deep breath. He couldn't go bursting in. He had to assess the situation. He felt Nicholas's hand on his arm. The man's face resembled a thundercloud. Jonas nodded and fell back. Nicholas stepped to the kitchen window and peered in. Jonas noted the front door was cracked and knew Brooke was in serious trouble. She would never leave her door open.

Nicholas stepped back and pulled his weapon from his holster. "He's got her tied up in the kitchen with a gun to her head."

Jonas felt his heart stop. The world around him simply froze. Then accelerated at warp speed. "What are we going to do?"

"Wait for backup."

"What if we don't have time to wait for them?"

Nicholas took another look. "We're going to have to create a distraction."

"How?"

"Knock on the door."

"And then what?"

"Get out of the way."

TWENTY

The knock on the door startled her. Her attacker jammed the gun against her head and she winced at the streak of lightning that arced through her skull. "Don't say a word," he growled.

"My car is sitting out front," she whispered. "My friends know I'm here. I'm late for a meeting and they're probably checking on me." She hadn't pulled into the garage that faced the front of the house. She'd just pulled in the drive and come in the front door.

He cursed. She stayed rock-still, her mind spinning. Who was out there? Gavin?

"Brooke? You in there?"

Nicholas. She glanced around for a weapon. The gun at her head was a slight deterrent, but not much. If she didn't act, she was dead. She knew it and the man next to her knew she knew it. But now she was a hostage. He needed her until he could get away. Which she would make sure didn't happen.

She kept her face toward the front door, hoping someone would glance in the kitchen window and be able to see her.

With the door that led to the garage at her attacker's

back, the only way out for her was going to have to be the front door.

"Get rid of whoever it is or they're dead, you understand me?"

"I understand."

"Brooke?" Nicholas called again.

"Yeah, Nicholas, what is it?"

"Are you all right?"

"Yes, late for my meeting with Gavin, but getting ready to head that way." She kept her voice as normal as possible, but speaking up for him to hear her sent pain vibrating through her brain. "I'll meet you there, okay?"

A loud crash ripped through the air and Brooke tensed as the man holding the gun went rigid. "What was that?"

"I don't know. Sounded like glass breaking," she said.

"Get up."

Brooke rose to her feet. The room spun, the nausea brought her to her knees and she fell, managing to roll to keep her head from taking another knock against the floor.

A shot sounded. Her attacker cried out. His weapon skidded to a stop in front of her and he jerked back, blood spreading across his left shoulder. He went to his knees.

She reached out to grab the gun. Her fingers skimmed across the grip but before she could close her hand around it, his palm swept her out of the way and once again, he had the Glock under control. He stood, his back to the kitchen door, the barrel aimed at her head. His finger twitched.

With a desperate cry, she rolled and heard the bullet slam into the hardwood next to her.

Another crash sounded, a scream of fury echoed

through the house. Brooke turned to see Jonas come through the garage door, eyes blazing, bat swinging.

A crack and then her attacker's cold eyes closed and he fell to the floor beside her.

Jonas dropped the bat he'd snagged from the neighbor's yard. He had broken the back window then raced around to the kitchen door just in time to see Brooke roll and a bullet slam beside her. Without pausing to think, he'd kicked the door in and swung the bat.

It had worked. She hadn't been shot, but her pale face, bleeding forehead and shallow breaths sent terror spiking through him. He dropped to the floor beside her. "Brooke? Brooke? Are you all right? Open your eyes. Talk to me."

"I'm okay," she said without opening her eyes.

"The ambulance is on the way," Nicholas said as he cuffed the still unconscious thug.

"He's not dead, is he?" Jonas felt queasy at the thought, then stiffened his spine. The man had tried to shoot Brooke and, by the grace of God, missed. He'd been about to pull the trigger again. What else could he have done?

Nicholas shook his head. "He's alive. He'll have a whopper of a headache, but he'll live." Nicholas sounded as though he regretted that fact.

"I didn't want to kill him, just stop him."

"Well, you did that." Officers swarmed the house. Nicholas gave him an admiring nod. "Nice job. A dangerous move, but you did it well." His jaw tightened. "If you'd waited, she would be dead, so I'm not going into all of the ways things could have gone wrong."

"All I cared about was getting to Brooke. I didn't really stop to think about it."

"It's probably best. When you stop to think too much,

it slows you down." He gave a Nicholas a smile and the unconscious thug a hard shove. "Wake up, you. Time to rise and shine and do some talking."

Chase and Gavin stepped inside and Jonas could see the intense concern for Brooke and himself. Gavin took one look at Brooke and frowned. "Stay put. I think the ambulance just pulled up."

"Who is he?" Brooke asked. She ignored Gavin and struggled into a sitting position. Jonas reached out to help her and then kept one hand on her shoulder in case she felt dizzy and started to keel over. She swayed, but stayed upright. He looked at the man on the floor, who'd started to stir, and wished he'd swung the bat a little harder.

Nicholas shook his head. "I don't know who he is." He patted him down. "No wallet or anything on him to give us a clue."

"He's starting to wake up," Gavin said. He shoved the man's shoulder. "Nap time is over. We need to talk." The man groaned and blinked. Gavin stood over him. "What's your name?"

"Shut up."

"Got a bit of a headache, I guess?" Brooke snapped.

Gavin pulled his iPhone from his pocket, hooked up the fingerprinting scanner and held it to the guy's index finger. "We'll know in a minute who you are if you're in the system."

The prisoner squirmed and yelled. Nicholas simply placed a foot in the middle of his back and held him down. With his hands behind his back, there wasn't much he could do. Jonas thought the officer was much too gentle.

Gavin looked up. "Damian Sharples."

"Priors?" Brooke asked.

"Oh, yes. A lot of them." Gavin kneeled to look the man in the face. "So, Mr. Sharples. Who hired you?"

"I need a doctor and a lawyer."

Gavin pinched his lips shut. Jonas could see his disgust. He nudged the man. "Where's my son?"

The thug's cold, empty eyes met his. "I don't know."

"You're a liar. Try again." Jonas kept his tone just as chilly.

Damian snarled. "If I knew where he was, he'd be dead."

Jonas drew back. And yet relief filled him. He really didn't know. And Felix wasn't dead. The sighting near Travis's house had encouraged him, but not laying eyes on Felix himself had kept him wondering. Had the officer really seen him? Maybe. Jonas wouldn't feel better until he had Felix back home.

"What about my dog?" Brooke asked. "You're the one who broke in and stole her. I know you know where she is."

"Yeah. I do. Good luck."

Jonas gripped Brooke's arm to keep her from going after the man. She fell back against him.

Brooke allowed the EMTs to bandage her head. However, when they tried to convince her to go to the hospital, she refused. "I know what a concussion feels like and I know what to do for it. I'll be fine."

Jonas disagreed and wanted to protest. He settled for a frown. She wrinkled her nose, but didn't budge on her decision. Jonas chanced a look at her boss, but Gavin simply shook his head and gave a small shrug as though to say not even he could force her if she refused.

Jonas grasped her hand and helped her to her feet. She

swayed and he slipped an arm around her and tucked her into his side. "You really should get checked out."

"If the symptoms don't subside in a day or so, I'll go to the doctor. For now, it's just a headache. The priority is finding Felix and Mercy."

"We'll take care of that," Nicholas said. "You need to go home and rest."

Brooke lifted her chin. "Damian Sharples may be in custody, but this case isn't over yet. Felix could still be in danger."

Jonas tensed. "But that guy said he didn't know where he was."

"That guy didn't, but someone else might."

TWENTY-ONE

Once Damian Sharples had been hauled away, Brooke put an ice pack on her head and downed a dose of ibuprofen. She would have preferred something a little stronger, but couldn't afford to feel drowsy. She had a kid and a dog to find.

Nicholas stepped back into the house. "Two officers picked up Felix's friend, Travis. They're waiting on us to come by and talk to him."

"The parents there?" Gavin asked.

"Yes."

"Let's go," Brooke said.

Gavin frowned. "Not you."

"I don't mean any disrespect, Gavin, but I'm going. I can ride with one of you or I can drive myself. It's important. I need to do this." She kept picturing Felix's face at the children's home. He'd opened up there, let go of his attitude and let his true self come out and shine for a bit. She'd seen so much potential in him in that short period of time. And he was Jonas's son. She wanted to see him safe.

Jonas stepped up beside her. "I'm coming, too."

Gavin's face turned red, but he gave a short nod.

"We're keeping it informal for now." The color faded from his cheeks and he rubbed his chin. "It actually might be a good idea to have you along, Jonas. They know and trust you."

"That's true."

"All right," Gavin said. "Nicholas, you and Chase head over to the Fuller home. Jonas and Brooke can follow. You guys stay out of sight and let Jonas see if he can get the information from the kid. If he doesn't have any luck, you can step in and put the pressure on."

Brooke walked past Gavin and out the door. Jonas stayed with her. He patted his pockets.

"You didn't drive, remember?" she said.

"Right." He held out his hand and she dropped her keys into it. "How's the head?"

"Hurts like crazy."

"I'm sorry."

She gave him a small smile. "It's all right. You got Sharples with a baseball bat. The fact that his head probably hurts worse than mine gives me great satisfaction."

Jonas climbed in the driver's seat, and Brooke slid into the passenger side. She leaned her head back and gave a small sigh. "I'm just going to keep my eyes closed while you drive, okay? Just follow Nicholas."

"Got it." He cranked the vehicle.

"Do you think Travis will tell you anything?"

"I have no idea, but I think he'll talk to me before he says anything to the police."

Silence fell between them. She could almost hear him thinking. "What is it?"

"Nothing."

"Something." She reached over and grasped his hand, just holding it, relishing the feel of his palm against hers.

She'd almost died today. She hadn't had time to process that thought. Now she could feel the shakes start to set in and tried to steel herself against them. She could fall apart later. Right now, she needed to be strong.

He lifted her hand to his lips and pressed a light kiss to her knuckles. She let her eyes flutter open and turned her head to watch him drive. "Something, Jonas. What is it?"

"I can feel you shaking."

"My adrenaline is crashing."

"I could have lost you today," he said. His voice was soft, but she heard the emotion behind the words, the hitch in his breath.

Her heart contracted. He didn't say, *You almost died today*. He'd said, *I could have lost you*. That sentence held so much more meaning than the other one.

She cleared her throat. "I've been in a lot of tight spots, but I'll admit, that was the tightest."

His fingers tightened around hers. "I understand that being in some danger comes with the territory, it's part of your job, but today…seeing you with the gun on your head—" He stopped and she saw his throat work.

"I know, Jonas. I'm sorry you had to see that. To go through that."

He whipped his gaze to hers for a brief moment before looking back at the road. "That's not it. Well, part of it, but seeing that, it brought home a lot of things for me."

"Like what?"

"Like…" He paused and sighed. "Like I want my son back. Now."

"I know." Her heart tumbled to her toes. And that surprised her. She'd wanted him to say something else. Spending time with him over the past week had hit home the fact that she'd never forgotten him—or moved on from him. She gasped.

"Are you all right?"

"Um, yeah. I just realized something, that's all."

"What?"

She looked up. "I'll tell you later. We're here."

Jonas led the way to the door. Nicholas and Brooke fell in behind him. He raised his hand to knock, but didn't need to. Charles opened the door and nodded. "Come on in." He took a look at Brooke's bandaged head. "Are you all right?"

"I'm fine. Just a little run-in with a bad guy and his gun. I'll heal," she murmured.

Jonas stepped inside and made his way into the living room. His heart beat a little faster. If Travis knew where Felix was, Jonas needed to rein in his anger and concentrate on just getting the boy to tell what he knew. Jonas took the couch. Brooke sat beside him. Travis shuffled into the room and slumped onto the wing-back chair near the fireplace.

"Tell them what you know, Travis," his father said. Anger vibrated beneath the surface. Travis's shoulders stiffened and his jaw hardened.

Jonas didn't need the man making things worse. "Travis, I just want to say I appreciate you being a good friend to Felix."

Travis's head shot up before he looked back down at the floor. He shrugged.

"Travis—" Charles stepped toward his son and Brooke rose and walked to the man.

She placed a hand on his arm. "Mr. Fuller, do you think I could have a glass of water?"

The man sighed, not fooled a bit by Brooke's manipulation. "Of course. I'll be right back."

"Thank you."

He left and Brooke returned to her seat with a nod for Jonas to continue.

Jonas cleared his throat. "Anyway, I just wanted to say that Felix really looks up to you and enjoys hanging out with you."

"He's the best friend I've ever had," Travis finally said.

"I know you want to protect him, but I really need to find him." Jonas's throat worked and he had to force the words out. "There are some pretty mean people after him and while we think we have one of them, it's possible the guy was working with someone and that they're still looking for Felix." Travis simply sat with his head hanging, the baseball cap shielding his face. "Travis, will you look me in the eye for a minute?" Travis hesitated, then looked up and Jonas snagged his gaze. The kid was completely conflicted. "If those guys get their hands on Felix, they'll kill him. It's that serious."

The indecision faded and Travis nodded. "And you can keep him safe?"

"As soon as we know he's not in the wrong hands, we have a plan to make sure they know that Felix doesn't have what they want. Once they know that, there's no reason for them to keep coming after him."

"He was afraid you were going to get hurt."

"What?" Jonas sat back.

"That's one of the reasons he took off. He was mad at you for wanting to send him away, sure, but he told me that maybe it was better if he just stayed away from you, then the people who were after him would leave you alone."

Jonas's breath left his lungs. A punch to his solar plexus wouldn't have had more effect than the boy's words. He swallowed and nodded. "I appreciate that. That means a lot to me, that he would do that, but we need to get him home and make sure he's protected. Please, Travis..."

"He's in my neighbor's tree house. Their kids are all grown up and they don't have any grandchildren, so I figured it would be a good place for him to hide out for a while. Just until things cooled down."

Jonas bolted to his feet. "He's there now?"

Travis nodded. "As far as I know."

Brooke laid a hand on Jonas's arm. "Take it easy. If you go charging out there, he might run."

"I won't charge." Jonas headed for the door. He wanted to see his son. He needed the tight ball of worry that had been his constant companion for the past few days to dissipate. And he needed to be able to tell Brooke exactly how he felt about her.

He stepped outside onto the back porch. The woods out back hid a lot. Including a tree house in the backyard of the neighbor to the right. The lack of a fence made for easy access. Heart pounding, palms sweating, Jonas headed for the woods. At the base of the tree, he looked up. "Felix?"

No answer. "I know you're up there, Felix. I talked to Travis. Will you please come down?" If Felix decided to stay quiet, Jonas would have to climb up. He'd placed one foot on the bottom rung of the ladder when Felix's head popped through the window.

"I can't believe Travis sold me out."

Jonas sighed. "He's trying to help you. Like we all are."

"I don't need any help and I'm not going to be sent away. I can take care of myself."

"You don't have to go away. You're not in danger anymore."

Felix fell silent, then his head disappeared. The small door opened and his son came down the ladder, as agile as a monkey. When he reached the bottom, Jonas reached out and pulled him into a hug.

Felix stood there for a moment, then Jonas felt his arms wrap around his waist. "You're not mad at me?" Felix mumbled into his chest.

"Oh, I'm mad, but I'm more glad than mad. So very glad you're safe. You scared me to death, son."

"I'm sorry. I really am. I just didn't want to go away and leave you all alone and not be able to make sure you were okay. Travis kept checking on you for me and letting me know that you were safe."

Jonas sighed and kissed the top of his son's head. "I understand. I'm not saying I'm okay with the way you went about everything, but I do understand."

Felix pulled back and looked up at him. "Really?"

"Really." He thought about the night he'd taken off after Brooke and shook his head. "Love makes you do dumb stuff sometimes."

"Love?"

"Yeah, love." Oh, boy. Yes, love. He cleared his throat. "I love you, Felix, you know that. And I know you were worried you'd brought those guys down on us because you took the phone."

Tears dripped down Felix's young face. He nodded. "I know. I was stupid. Still am, but you know I love you, too."

"Yeah," Jonas whispered. "I know. And you're thirteen. I suppose you're going to do some stupid things over the next few years. Let's just make sure they don't get you killed, okay?"

"Or you," Felix mumbled.

Nicholas stepped up and Brooke was only two steps behind him. "Were you in that tree house when Max was trying to track you?" Nicholas asked.

Felix pulled away from his dad. "Yes."

Nicholas frowned. "I guess Max and I need to do some more training."

Felix gave a small smile. "It wasn't totally his fault. I figured someone would try to track me with the dogs so I changed into one of Travis's shirts and had him drag mine along the ground, then get on his bike and ride with it flapping in the wind. I didn't know if it would work or not, but figured it was worth a try."

Admiration glinted in Nicholas's eyes for a brief moment before he shook his head and looked at Jonas. "Smart kid."

"Too smart," Jonas muttered.

Brooke's phone rang. She answered it and relief crossed her face. She looked at him. "They found Mercy."

"Wonderful."

He nudged his son. "Come on, let's go tell Travis everything's fine."

"His dad's going to kill him."

"Naw, he's mad, but I don't think he'll do Travis any bodily harm. Might ground him for a year or two..."

Felix smiled and wrapped an arm around Jonas's waist as they headed back to the house together. Brooke walked beside them. Jonas reached out and grasped her fingers.

"Now what?" Felix asked.

"Now I go greet a prodigal of my own," Brooke said.

Chase and Isaac met her at her home. Chase opened the back of his SUV and Mercy bounded out.

"Mercy!" Brooke called. She raced over to her friend and partner and dropped to her knees. The dog gave her a sloppy kiss and Brooke didn't even care. Tears filled her eyes and ran down her cheeks. She knew she shouldn't be so attached to the animal, but her heart had been lost from the day they became partners. She looked up at Chase and Isaac. "Where did you find her?"

"Damian's house. He had her tied up in a shed out back."

Felix climbed from the car. Mercy trotted over to him and gave him a wet greeting, too. Felix simply laughed and patted the dog's head. Mercy went to the front door and sat. Brooke laughed. "I guess she wants to go in." She opened the door and Mercy beelined it for her bed in front of the fireplace. She snagged her bone, settled it between her paws and started chewing.

"She's glad to be home," Jonas said.

"I'm glad she's home," Brooke agreed. She looked at Felix. "And I'm very glad you're all right."

Felix looked away then back at Brooke. He gave her a small smile. "That makes two of us."

Chase clapped Isaac on the shoulder. "We've got a meeting in thirty."

Isaac nodded. "We'd better head out."

Brooke frowned. "Is it the whole team?"

"Yes."

"Then I'd better get ready."

"Whoa, wait a minute," Chase said. "That was a hard crack on the head. You're supposed to be taking it easy."

"Says who?"

"Gavin."

She sighed. “I’m fine. I need to be in on the meeting. I’ll meet you guys there.”

“I’ll bring her,” Jonas said. He looked at Brooke. “You don’t need to be driving, so we’ll just remove that from your list. If you have your mind made up to go, I’ll take you.”

Isaac clapped Jonas on the back and looked at Brooke. “He knows you. Impressive. You’d better hang on tight to this one.”

“Go away,” she said, her tone mild.

Isaac laughed.

Jonas looked at Felix. “I guess you’re coming with us.”

“Ugh. Do I have to?”

Before Jonas could respond, Isaac said, “Why don’t I have an officer drop him at his buddy’s house and stay with him until we’re done with your meeting?”

“Yes,” Felix begged. “Please.”

“That’s fine.” Jonas nodded and Felix punched a fist into the air. Isaac made the arrangements and Felix got his stuff together.

After they left, Brooke looked at Jonas and the tender look in his eyes was nearly her undoing. She didn’t want to go to the meeting, she wanted to stay home, take some more medication and then snuggle down into Jonas’s arms while Felix played with Mercy.

Instead, she drew in a deep breath. “I’m ready when you are.”

Jonas led the way to the car and she climbed in. Mercy hopped in the back with Felix. Brooke kept stealing glances at him as he drove, his hands strong and sure on the wheel, his gaze alert as he watched the other drivers. He shot her a glance and caught her watching him.

A smile slid across his lips. "You never did tell me what you realized."

"What?"

"Earlier, you said you realized something and then said you'd tell me later." He shrugged. "It's later."

Brooke bit her lip, then stiffened her spine. She'd made a mistake eight years ago. It was time to do things right. "You asked me why I'd never married."

"Right. You said your career was your focus."

"That's what I said. That's what I had convinced myself I believed, too."

"Huh?"

"Jonas, the reason I never married is because—" Did she dare? Her heart pounded and her palms started to sweat.

"Because?"

"Because of the fact that I can't have children, yes, but also because I just couldn't find another…you."

His breath caught and he pulled to the side of the road. "I can't just let you walk into a meeting as though you didn't just say that. You're going to be a little late."

She nodded, shrugged and couldn't stop the little laugh that escaped. "It's okay. I'm always a little late. They expect it by now."

"Tell me what you meant by that last statement."

"I dated a few guys after we went our separate ways. I even got up the nerve to tell one of them that I couldn't have children."

"And he dumped you?"

The leashed violence in the words almost made her smile. She shook her head. "He said it didn't matter, that we could always adopt. He himself was adopted and he'd always hoped the woman he married would be open to going through the process with him."

"Oh."

"I was stunned. I'd already planned my reaction, steeled myself for when he walked away." She spread her hands and blinked back the tears. "And then…he didn't."

"So what was the problem?"

"I realized at that very moment that I didn't love him. I wanted to. I tried. But I just didn't. But his reaction made me sick to my stomach, too."

"I'm confused."

She gave a small hiccupping laugh. "I know. When he said that we could adopt, it hit me that I should have told you. I started playing the what-if game. I nearly drove myself crazy. I told myself I'd hurt you enough and that I didn't deserve you. So, I threw myself into my work and did my best to forget you," she whispered. "But I couldn't. Because I loved you. I've always loved you, Jonas. I've never stopped and I'm so sorry for hurting you and I hope you can forgive—"

He kissed her. He wrapped his hand around the back of her neck and gently pulled her closer. She went still, her brain whirling. Then told it to shut up and kissed him back. An I-missed-you-I'm-so-glad-to-be-back-with-you kind of kiss. When he finally pulled away, Brooke had to concentrate on breathing. Her face felt hot, flushed. "Wow."

"Yeah. Double wow." He blinked, stared at her for a few seconds then shook his head. "Wow." He cranked the car. "Let's get you to your meeting. I'll be waiting outside when you're done and we'll finish this conversation."

"Right."

"And tell everyone that they're invited to a cookout at my house tomorrow night."

"A cookout?"

He shrugged. "For those who can make it. Everyone has really put their lives on hold—some even on the line—for me and Felix. I'd like to do something for you all."

She nodded. "All right, I'll pass the word."

"Oh, and one more thing."

"What?"

"I love you, too."

Fifteen minutes later, Brooke slipped into her chair and ignored the good-natured teasing of the guys. She barely heard them as she replayed the kiss over and over in her mind. The kiss, the words, the look on his face…

Fiona entered the conference room and Brooke shifted into a more comfortable position. The bandage on her left temple made the skin under the tape itch, but she resisted scratching it.

"Do we know anything about the guy we caught at Brooke's house?" Chase asked.

"Not much," Fiona said. "He's got a nice rap sheet that includes armed robbery and assault with a deadly weapon. However, I did find one interesting thing."

"What's that?" Gavin asked.

"He was in rehab for a while. He completed the program, got out and got a job."

"Where?"

"He worked in the janitorial department of Thorne Industries."

Brooke sat up straight as she processed that bomb.

"Which means we can tie him to Congressman Jeffries," Nicholas muttered.

Gavin shot him a dark look. Nicholas didn't look away.

Isaac tapped the table. "So is he talking?"

"No," Gavin said. "Not a word. Said someone called him and asked if he needed some fast, easy cash. He said yes and the person gave him his instructions. He has no idea who the voice on the other end was."

"Of course not," Brooke said.

"But we can tie him to the aide's death. We found Paul Harrison's wallet in Damian's apartment."

"Excellent," Brooke murmured.

"Any word on Erin Eagleton?" Gavin asked.

"Nothing," Chase said, his jaw tight, eyes narrowed. "We'll find her, though."

"It's possible she's dead," Nicholas said.

"She's not dead." Chase's voice rose a fraction and the room went silent. Chase cleared his throat. "Sorry. I just don't believe she's dead or that she had anything to do with the shootings. She'll explain when we find her."

Brooke again noted the hope, the faith in Chase's voice and wondered at his relationship with Erin—who'd been Michael Jeffries's girlfriend.

"Then we need to hope she turns up soon. I'm ready to solve this case. Any more on the internet service provider trackings?" A few weeks ago, someone researching bills introduced by Congressman Jeffries had been tracked to rural Virginia. The research had gone all the way back to his first term.

Chase exhaled and shook his head. "No, nothing since then. If it's Erin, she's gone quiet."

"We've made a statement to the press that we've found the phone and that we're pulling information from it.

Hopefully, that will deter whoever hired Mr. Sharples to go after Felix."

"He should be safe now," Nicholas agreed.

"Good," Gavin said. "Now…"

Brooke fidgeted and Gavin's voice faded. Jonas was waiting on her and she wanted to finish their conversation. Hope made her giddy and unable to totally focus on the conversation around her. She just wanted to take a break, to go be with Jonas.

"You okay, Brooke? Do you need to take off?"

She blinked at Gavin's question. She touched the bandage on her forehead. Then stood. "Yes, I think I do." For more reasons than one.

Gavin nodded. "Someone will call you with an update."

"Great." She walked toward the exit then turned. "Oh, you're all invited to a cookout at Jonas's house tomorrow night at five-thirty." She slipped out of the conference room, a smile spreading across her lips.

TWENTY-TWO

Brooke looked around. The cookout was a huge success. How Jonas had managed to put this together so fast, she'd never know. Probably had a caterer for a client who owed him a favor. Burgers and hot dog smoke filled the air and her nose twitched while her stomach rumbled.

Everyone had been able to make the cookout, including Cassie and Gavin, Adam and Lana, Nicholas and even Chase who refused to give up the search for Erin Eagleton. He kept looking at his phone and she knew he was hoping Fiona would have something for him to work with. So far, there was nothing.

All the dogs were in attendance and behaved perfectly in spite of the tempting aromas that drifted past them.

Jonas was dressed in a ridiculous apron that said Real Men Wear Aprons. He kept shooting her secret smiles and she figured she'd never need to use makeup on her cheeks again.

Felix's attitude had changed overnight and he and Jonas seemed to have turned a corner in their relationship. Last night, she'd left them alone to give them time to talk even though she wanted to be with Jonas. He needed to be with his son and she was all right with that.

Nicholas stepped up beside her. "How's the head?"

She touched the bandage she'd just changed that morning. "Still aching, but nothing some ibuprofen and I can't handle."

"I'm glad." He paused and took a sip of his tea, his eyes on Jonas, who threw a football to Felix. "You love him, don't you?"

She sighed. "Yes. I do."

"He's a good man. I approve."

She laughed. "Thanks. That actually means a lot." She sobered. "How's it going with Selena Barrows?"

He shook his head. "She's a feisty one, no doubt about that. She's desperate to find her cousin and pushes me on a daily basis about our progress, but clearly Erin's not too keen on being found."

"Do you think she's still alive?"

"I hope so because I think she's the only one who knows what happened the night Michael Jeffries was killed and his father, the congressman, shot and left for dead."

"Besides the murderer."

"Exactly," he murmured.

She caught Jonas's eye. "Excuse me."

Nicholas smiled. "Of course. I wouldn't want to get in the way of true love."

She punched Nicholas in the arm and made her way over to Jonas. "You don't need an apron, you're not cooking."

"I know, but Felix gave it me for my birthday a couple of months ago and I figured now was a good time to test drive it."

He stole her heart in so many ways. "You're a wonderful dad, Jonas."

He leaned over to place a light kiss on her lips. The crowd faded away. "I love you, Brooke. I feel like I've loved you forever. How do you feel about adoption?"

She blinked. "As you can imagine, I've thought about it a lot. Why?"

"So you've thought about it. Does that mean you're open to it?"

She gave a small laugh. "Of course. Are you?"

"That's why I'm asking. I think you'd be a great mother."

Tears surfaced. She blinked them back. "Thanks, Jonas. I like to think I would."

"So, do you want to adopt some kids?"

She wasn't slow. She caught the meaning behind his words. "I think that would be lovely. One day."

"One day…soon?"

"Possibly. That depends."

"On what?"

"On how soon the father of those adopted kids wants to adopt."

"He wants to pretty soon, I'm sure."

"How can you be so sure?"

Jonas glanced over his shoulder and she saw him wink at Felix who seemed to have a boundless amount of energy. He bounced on the balls of his feet. At his dad's wink, his eyes went wide. He shoved a hand in his pocket and pulled out a whistle. Jonas nodded. Felix blew the whistle. Everyone went quiet.

Felix said, "I have an announcement to make." He looked at Jonas. "Actually my dad has a question to ask."

Brooke looked at Jonas. He swallowed hard and gave a small laugh. "Okay, maybe I shouldn't have invited all these people because I'm really nervous now," he whispered. "But, oh well." He dropped to his knee and a soft gasp escaped her.

The crowd stayed silent.

"Jonas?"

Indecision flickered in his eyes. "Is it too soon?"

And Brooke knew. She had no doubts. Jonas was the man she would marry. "No, it's not too soon."

His brilliant smile flashed at her. "Brooke, it's been a long time coming, but—" he took a deep breath "—I love you. Will you marry me and fill up our house with Felix and a bunch of other kids from the children's home?"

She didn't hesitate. "Yes," she whispered. "A thousand times yes."

Felix whooped. Clapping and cheers broke out. Jonas lowered his lips to hers and gave her a thoroughly approving kiss. Then he swept her off her feet and swung her around in a circle. When he placed her back on her feet, Mercy bounded over and barked. Jonas scratched her ears and Felix dropped to the ground to hug her. When Felix stood, he looked up at Brooke and gave her a shy smile. "Does this mean I get to call you Mom?"

"You don't have to, but I would be honored for you to call me Mom if it's what you want," she said.

"I want." He blinked rapidly and sniffed, then stepped forward to wrap her in a hug. "Thanks…Mom."

Brooke had to clear her throat before she could speak. And she could only squeak out, "You bet…son."

Felix released her. Jonas looked like he might join in the crying fest, but then people started in on the congratulations and Brooke found her tears gone, laughter taking their place. After a few minutes, she flung herself back in Jonas's arms. "Thank you."

"I should be the one thanking you. You've made Felix

and me complete now." He took her left hand in his and slipped a beautiful diamond on her ring finger. "I've had that ring for a long time."

"I don't know what to say," she whispered.

"Say you'll stay with me forever."

She nodded through the tears that had surfaced once again. "I'll stay. Forever."

Another kiss followed another hug, with his arms wrapped tight around her and her head nestled against his healing shoulder.

She sighed and sent up a thankful prayer. She was right where she wanted to be.

Forever.

* * * * *

If you liked this CAPITOL K-9 UNIT *novel,*
watch for the next book,
SECURITY BREACH by Margaret Daley,
available June 2014.

And don't miss a single story in the
CAPITOL K-9 UNIT *miniseries:*

Book #1: PROTECTION DETAIL by Shirlee McCoy
Book #2: DUTY BOUND GUARDIAN by Terri Reed
Book #3: TRAIL OF EVIDENCE by Lynette Eason
Book #4: SECURITY BREACH by Margaret Daley
Book #5: DETECTING DANGER by Valerie Hansen
Book #6: PROOF OF INNOCENCE by Lenora Worth

Dear Reader,

Thank you for coming along with me on Jonas and Brooke's journey to catch the bad guy and find love along the way. I so enjoyed getting to know the characters. All Jonas wanted was to keep his son safe and convince Brooke he was the guy for her in spite of the pain of the past. Brooke had to learn that sometimes playing it safe isn't always what God wants us to do. Sometimes He'll ask us to step out of our comfort zones in order to complete the tasks He has for us—and to receive the blessings He wants to bestow. As I wrote this story, I was reminded that I need to do that. To take risks, step out of my comfort zone, see what God has planned for me. I want to encourage you to do that, as well!

If you've enjoyed this story, I'd love for you to let me know that. My email is lynetteeason@lynetteeason.com. My website is www.lynetteeason.com and you can also find me on Facebook (www.facebook.com/lynette.eason) and Twitter (@lynetteeason). I look forward to hearing from you!

God Bless,

Lynette Eason

COMING NEXT MONTH FROM
Love Inspired® Suspense

Available June 2, 2015

SECURITY BREACH
Capitol K-9 Unit • by Margaret Daley

A White House trespasser is on the loose, and tour director Selena Barrow teams up with Capitol K-9 Unit member Nicholas Cole and his trusted dog, Max, to track down the intruder...before his destructive plans are brought to fruition.

EXIT STRATEGY
Mission: Rescue • by Shirlee McCoy

Widow Lark Porter's set on finding her late husband's murderers—but she's quickly taken captive. Former army ranger Cyrus Mitchell will risk everything to rescue Lark...and bring her captors to justice.

BACKFIRE
Mountain Cove • by Elizabeth Goddard

Since testifying against a gang leader, Tracy Murray's been hiding as an Alaskan search and rescuer. When the crime boss's henchmen find her, Tracy turns to firefighter David Warren—who'll stop at nothing to keep her safe.

PAYBACK
Echo Mountain • by Hope White

Nia Sharpe's world is turned upside down when her estranged brother suddenly visits—with a dangerous drug cartel tailing him. Though her military veteran boss, Aiden McBride, acts as her protector, it also means he has become the criminals' next target.

PERMANENT VACANCY • by Katy Lee

Television host Colm McCrae doesn't know whether "accidents" keep occurring on set of Gretchen Bauer's B&B restoration because his boss is desperate to boost ratings—or because someone is out for revenge against the beautiful woman.

COVERT JUSTICE • by Lynn Huggins Blackburn

FBI agent Heidi Zimmerman has had enough of an infamous crime family's deadly schemes—it's time for her to go undercover. She knows two things—they're after Blake Harrison, and Heidi may be his only hope for survival.

LOOK FOR THESE AND OTHER LOVE INSPIRED BOOKS WHEREVER BOOKS ARE SOLD, INCLUDING MOST BOOKSTORES, SUPERMARKETS, DISCOUNT STORES AND DRUGSTORES.

LISCNM0515